OTHER BOOKS BY NATALIE SAVAGE CARLSON

Sailor's Choice

Sailor's Choice

by Natalie Savage Carlson

Pictures by George Loh

HARPER & ROW, PUBLISHERS
NEW YORK

U. S. 1462759

For Dan

Contents

Sailor's Choice

My neighbor William Sacrey, a former Newfoundlander, furnished me with most of the anecdotes which have been developed into the incidents of this story. He went on three sealing expeditions in the early part of the century and lived in such an outport as my fictional Spanish Choice Cove. Even the dog Sailor, as named and described, was his boyhood pet in a district where dogs were not allowed.

I

Visitors

"There are few of his kind left on their own native island," said Captain Heber Wight, looking down at the great black dog sprawled near his feet. "If you want to find his likes anywhere now, you have to go to the kennels of England."

"Then maybe that's where he ought to go," countered the dog constable. "You rightly knew when you brought him here that dogs aren't allowed in Spanish Choice Cove because of the sheep. A man keeping sheep doesn't want them molested by vicious dogs."

The captain's broad face above his square-cut beard bloated with anger, and his unruly eyebrows twitched. "I want to see the man who'll call Sailor a vicious dog to his face or mine," he declared. "And any time Sailor harms one of the village sheep, I'll pay the price of all the sheep in the cove."

The two men faced each other in the parlor of the captain's house. Both were stone-stubborn Newfoundlanders. Back in

1

the nineteen-twenties it was said that men of this crown colony were made of iron and oak.

"Now, Captain Wight," demurred the constable, "we've been friends a long time. Our fathers sailed to the Grand Banks on the same schooner and there's never been any trouble between our families. But you've got to get rid of the dog."

"Too bad *you* didn't stick to the fishing too, Constable Cotter," retorted the captain.

"But I didn't," the other reminded him. "And I don't make the laws. I only see that they get kept, because I'm the constable for the east side of this bay. If it was anybody else but you, sir, I'd fine him and carry off the dog myself. But I'll give you time to find a new home for him."

"And if it was anybody else but you, sir," snapped the captain, "I'd say it's a low, mean chucklehead who'd give up fishing to go nosing around the coves looking for dogs to persecute."

"It isn't my law," repeated Constable Cotter.

"You're enforcing it," insisted the captain, "but I'll abide by it. You know I'm taking the *Polar Star* down the Labrador coast with the sealing fleet in March. Only two weeks off it is. Give me that time, William Cotter, and I'll take the dog to sea with me. I'll find him a new master among my crew. It isn't every man lucky enough to get an old-time Newfoundland dog that can work like a horse and think like a man."

They both looked at the dog. Sailor seemed to realize that he was the cause of the trouble. He had flattened his black hulk against the floor as if to make himself as inconspicuous as possible. His chin was pressed so closely to the carpet that

2

his ears fell over his paws. But his brown eyes rolled from man to man as if he were trying to understand their words.

"Granted, Captain," agreed Constable Cotter after a moment's pause, "and it's a good master I'm hoping you find for him."

"And if I don't," growled Captain Wight, "be cripes, I'll jerk up this house and sail it across the line to another anchorage where dogs are legal."

"I believe you would," said the constable.

The men shook hands.

"Now that the nasty business is over," said the captain, "how about a cup of tea, William? It's cold as a seal's scutters outside, and you've got a long ride back to Sample's Harbour in that open sleigh box."

"No, thanks, Heber," replied the constable. "If I stayed another two minutes, you might talk me into letting you keep the dog here. He *is* a handsome, noble beast and a pride to the cove. More so than those baa-baa sheep, by jiggs."

The dog constable pulled his coat together and buttoned it down the front. He put the fleece-lined elsinor back on his head and pulled the flaps down over his ears, then slid his crooked fingers into the sealskin mittens.

The dog slowly rose to his paws, revealing the white spot on his chest—like a handkerchief neatly tucked into a breast pocket of his shiny coat.

He followed the men to the door. Captain Wight opened it and an arctic blast blew into the house. As the constable stepped through the doorway the dog squeezed between the men and went lumbering down the road. His oily black hair was as dense and weather-resistant as a duck's feathers. He could not stand the heat of the house very long.

He went down the icy steps and began his daily round of the snow-blanketed district.

Sailor had been whelped at sea by the ship's dog of the fishing schooner *Thaddeus* during one of the worst storms that ever stamped in from the northeast. The skipper had given the young dog to Captain Wight when their ships had gone on dock together for the summer at Heart's Content. For almost a year Sailor had lived peacefully at Spanish Choice Cove. He had been a help to Mrs. Wight, pulling groceries home from the store in the little red wagon and guarding the premises. He didn't play favorites with her or the captain.

But he was contraband in this community where dogs were not allowed, and only his good nature and his popularity with the villagers had kept him from the notice of the dog constable so long.

Sailor walked with the rolling sea gait of his master. The wind scarcely riffled his flat coat. The icy air was turned into vapor by his powerful lungs.

He followed the cleared road that led to the village. It was a jumble of houses clinging to the rocky cliffs like the nests of seabirds. Only plumes of smoke rising over the flat roofs gave proof of human presence.

Below were the fishing platforms and sheds, and the rickety wharf. The flakes, which were covered with drying cod during the summer months, lay bare except for the ragged coverlets of snow over them.

The sheltered water at the bottom of the launching ramp was frozen into an icy sheet. Even the steep, winding paths cleared about the small blocklike houses were deserted. And the sheep that grazed on the ridges during the summer were penned inside the barns behind some of the houses. No one family owned more than two or three, so there was no need for a herd dog.

The sole sign of life was the constable's sleigh disappearing over the ridge road.

Sailor turned up the road that led past a sweep of stunted tamaracks. Then he struck out for the rise that separated Spanish Choice from the cove next to it. The dog stopped at the summit, and his eyes swept the white hollow below him.

5

He gave a joyous bark and went bounding down the other side.

The figure of a man was making its way toward the cliffs closing in the arm of water. Sailor knew that the long stick reaching above his shoulder was a gun.

The hunter was shapeless as a furled sail in his canvas jacket and woolen trousers. He welcomed Sailor with a heavy pat on his neck.

"Good day to you, Sailor man," he said. "You're just the partner I need when the hounds are flying. I've heard you are a good retriever."

Tom Boggan was a strapping young man who had recently moved from a southerly outport to the fishing village at Spanish Choice. Although he was unmarried, he could boast a large family because it included his parents and his older brother's wife and children.

The pair climbed the backside of a cliff toward a gully which sheltered them from the wind and hid them from the birds' sharp eyes. Tom sat down on the packed snow and looked at his single-barreled shotgun.

Man and dog patiently awaited the coming of the old squaw ducks. The wind died down and the waters in the inlet smoothed. Then they saw a small flock approaching from the sea in jerky flight. As they came closer their plaintive cries of *conker-leeker, conker-leeker* floated up the narrow inlet.

Sailor began to quiver with excitement as he watched the ducks flying low over the water. As if on signal, they plummeted below the surface to feed on the bottom.

The hunter stood erect and braced the gun against his shoulder. When black heads began breaking water, he pulled the trigger. The alarmed ducks took flight, winging away with the speed of shot. But two lifeless bodies remained behind, floating far out among the ice cakes.

Sailor needed no command. He raced along the cliff to a spot above clear water. Although it was fully twenty feet down, he leaped through the air to the water below. His webbed paws paddled toward the closer bird. He seized it in his strong jaws, then made for the reach of shore to the left. Ignoring the hunter, he headed for the rise beyond the hollow.

"Here, Sailor!" shouted Tom, holding out his hand. "Come, boy! Bring me the hound."

Suddenly he remembered the experiences of others who had used this retriever. Sailor would give the bird to no one, not even to the captain had he been there. He would carry it back to the Wight house and lay it at the front door. From there it belonged to anyone who cared to claim it.

The dog took a shortcut over the snow-crusted hills, the duck's long tail hanging from his jaws. He swung into the road again and past the scattered country dwellings. He went loping through the village and down the road to Captain Wight's square yellow house with its green corners and roof. There he laid the bird at the front door. He sat down on his haunches to await the hunter's arrival.

It was almost twenty minutes before he saw the man with the shotgun trudging along the Spanish Choice road. Tom Boggan climbed the hill to the Wight house.

"You old rogue!" he scolded Sailor. "It'll be a hot day at the North Pole the next time I go hunting with you."

He stamped the snow from his boots, then knocked at the

7

door. Mrs. Wight answered it. She was a short woman, and the black shawl gripped winglike above her white apron gave her the appearance of a plump puffin.

"Oh, it's you, Tom Boggan," she said. "A good day to you, and come on in. The captain will enjoy seeing you, and you look as if you need a hot drink."

Tom doffed his cap and returned her greeting. "I've come to make a complaint, ma'am," he said with a grin. "Some rogue stole my cock hound, and I had a suspicion I'd find it here."

As Tom spoke the captain's husky figure appeared in the doorway. "Come in and welcome, me lad," he cried, "and what's that fine cock hound doing at my door?"

"It may be your door," retorted Tom, "but it's my hound."

Mrs. Wight, standing in the shelter of the captain's broad back, began to shiver. "Heber, you go out or, Tom, you come in," she ordered, "but don't stand there with the door open chilling the whole house."

"Come in, come in," roared Captain Wight. "You can pick up your bird when you leave. You come in too, Sailor," he ordered.

But Sailor slowly padded down the road. He had remembered the other duck floating in the water.

As Tom entered the narrow hall and set his gun down carefully in the umbrella rack his eyes wandered over the flooring and walls. "Good carpentry," he remarked, "and good timber."

"Each deserves the other," said the captain, "Would you believe I built this house with my own hands when I was your age? Didn't know too much about putting a house together,

8

but I'd had experience building boats. So that's the way I built her. Shipshape and watertight as a lobster shell."

He gave the wall a strong thump, and the sound was muffled by density.

"I came here as a bride," put in Mrs. Wight, "and I was mighty proud to move in. The captain had made the kitchen handy as a ship's galley. Of course he wasn't a master then, and he wanted to build me a bigger house when he got his papers, but I wouldn't have any other home. It's just right for two."

They entered the parlor, and Tom went over to the stove. It still threw off heat from the fire built for the constable's visit. The young man rubbed his hands together briskly.

"It was only day before yesterday that Sailor brought home a fine bottlenose duck," said Captain Wight. "Just what Sarah needed for the new feather bed she's filling. But old Uncle Charlie Butler turned up and claimed it." Then his manner sobered. "I'm going to miss having Sailor around," he continued. "He's a great dog, but my last caller in this parlor was the dog constable. The honorable William Cotter says I have to get rid of him."

Tom clucked his tongue against his teeth in sympathy.

"I'd sure like to take him myself if I didn't live in the same district," he said. "The children are afraid of him because he's so big, but they'd soon get used to him if he belonged to me."

Tom's little nephews and nieces had always run screaming at the sight of the great black beast.

Mrs. Wight interrupted them with the tea that the constable

9

had declined. The men sat down and the captain balanced his saucer on his knee.

"What will you do about Sailor?" Tom asked, after taking his first sip.

"I'll try to find him a master among the men on my ship," said Captain Wight. "Somebody who doesn't live in a restricted district. But my problem is more immediate. I'm all set to take the train to St. John's to join the ship, but I don't know how I will manage with such a big dog as a passenger."

"No train problem for me," said the younger man, "I'm taking the horse to pull the sled with my sea chest and sleeping bag. And I'm hoping my brother will get back from the mill in time to go with me and drive the horse home. I'm sure grateful to you for giving me a berth on the *Polar Star.*"

Captain Wight set the cup and saucer down on the table and brushed away the gratitude with a wave of his hand. "It's me grateful to find another dependable man for my crew," he said, "but, be cripes, Tom, don't bother your brother with this. You take Sailor to pull your sled to St. John's. We'll come home by the bay schooner and bring the sled back that way."

Tom Boggan lowered his tea cup. "It's a bargain, sir," he agreed. "I'll even throw in the cock hound so Mrs. Wight can get her feather bed done."

"No, you take the bird with you, me boy," the captain insisted. "You shot it."

Tom Boggan finished his tea with a gurgling swallow. He thanked Mrs. Wight for the tea before going outside. He picked up his duck, then set out for the fishing village.

10

Sailor came loping toward Tom with the other bird in his jaws. It was a short-tailed hen.

"A fine brace they'd make," Tom spoke aloud.

He stopped in the road and laid his gun down. "Come, Sailor," he coaxed, trying to block the dog's way. "Give me the hound."

The fingers in his gloves curved and his knees were bent outward. Man and dog zigzagged back and forth in a taglike contest. Each time Tom made a lunge to snag the duck, Sailor dodged him. Finally the dog outwitted the man by making a play to the right, then quickly dashing past on the unguarded left side.

Tom Boggan muttered under his breath as he watched Sailor streak up the road toward home.

"Tell the captain that's one for the feather bed," he called after him.

II

Off to the Icefields

St. John's, the oldest town in North America, was built solidly on the hills around its cliff-hugged harbor. Great Edwardian buildings of three and four stories crowded against the streets. A fog of coal smoke spread over the chimney pots of their flat roofs.

The old seaport was in a holiday mood as Tom Boggan trudged down Water Street with Sailor pulling the loaded sled behind him. Seal hunters from all over the big island were swarming into town to join their ships. They swaggered like pirates in their high boots, with sculping knives hanging from the belts that cinched their waists. They gathered in groups on the sidewalk, these rugged men in canvas jackets and slouched caps. The strange nasal dialect of men from the northern outports filled the frosty air. They talked of nogg-heads and ballycatters, bedlamers and jinkers—words alien to Tom's ears.

Sailor was only one of many beasts slogging through the slush of the cobbled street. Shaggy island ponies were drawing their masters' sea chests and sacks toward the wharves. Great-shouldered horses with heavy hoofs pulled low drays loaded with boxes and barrels.

Little yapping "crackies," as small dogs were called, ran loose with no collars or responsibilities. One of them, a scrappy little mongrel, challenged Sailor's right to the street. He came growling at him with gray hair on end and yellow fangs bared.

"Go away! Begone!" ordered Tom, reaching for the club on his sled. But Sailor had his own means of defense. As the crackie leaped at him he slapped him down with one giant paw. Then with the same paw he held the little dog helpless against the curb.

After a few snarling struggles the crackie began yelping his defeat. Sailor released his hold, and the vanquished dog went racing away among the boots of the crowd.

A group of Northmen standing on the nearby corner burst into raucous laughter. One of them shouted, "He'll shule come arn big dog now."

Tom smiled back, as he could understand the meaning of the remark if not the words. Then he stopped Sailor while he paused to look through the plate glass of a store window.

In the center was a stuffed gray seal whose pelt was marked with black bands roughly shaped like a harp. Equipment for the hunt was displayed around it: heavy gaff hooks on long poles for dealing the death blow on the noses of the young seals, the "whitecoats"; shiny rifles for shooting the nimble

13

adults; and razor-bladed sculping knives for slitting the skin and layer of fat from the dead animals.

Tom's eyes slid covetously over the merchandise.

An urchin approached. He was a thin whip of a boy with a marmalade-colored forelock hanging under the visor of the cap that was too big for him. His blue eyes widened at sight of the big dog hitched to the sled.

"Cricky, he's a big one," said the boy "I've never seen such a big dog before."

Although other children along the way had drawn back from a dog of such size, the boy stepped up to Sailor and fearlessly ran his hand over his black coat. Then he turned his attention to the wealth of equipment in the window.

"Cricky, mister," he exclaimed, "I wish I could buy all that gear. Then I'd be sure they'd take me sealing."

Tom laughed. "Every boy in Newfoundland wants to sail with the sealing fleet," he said. "I hear that in the old days the captains would take them, but now the only ones who make it are the stowaways. They say the *Vargo* sailed last year with twelve of them hidden away."

The boy's eyes grew bigger and bigger as he listened to Tom's words.

"You going with them?" he asked.

"Yes," said Tom. "Me and the dog. But my heart's really in fishing. I hope to make enough money to buy a trap net so I'll have my own and not have to work for others."

He slowly turned from the window, touched his cap in farewell to the boy, and urged Sailor on. They went down a narrow side street that led to the wharf. The boy followed at a distance.

14

The wharf was even more crowded with sealers. Sailor had to lace his way between more drays and sleds, baskets of coal and giant cans of blasting powder. A flock of little boys, noisy and lively as the gulls over the harbor, were running from ship to ship. Some of the bolder ones broke away to board the sealing vessels and climb the ratlines.

The steamers were flying the flags of their houses. There was the *Polar Star* just a stone's throw away. She was a black three-masted schooner of honorable age, equipped with a steam engine as well as the sails, which added to her speed when the wind was up.

Captain Wight met them at the gangway with a slap on the back for Tom Boggan and an equally hearty one for Sailor's head. The captain looked like an old seal himself in his long fur coat and shaggy cap.

"Any trouble along the way?" he asked.

"None at all, sir," replied Tom. "The coves were frozen solid and Sailor was better than any horse. I didn't have to guide him."

Captain Wight helped Tom loose the traces, then led him and Sailor across the gangway. A couple of obliging men followed with the sled. The captain gave it a quick look.

"I see you've brought your sleeping sack, and I hope there are raw onions in the chest. They give you greater lung power out on the ice."

"They ought to give me a stronger breath anyway," quipped Tom. "I don't think I forgot anything, sir. My mother even made me take clean shirts and extra socks."

"You won't need them on the *Polar Star*," explained the captain. "And what you do wear here, you'll want to bury in the

15

ground when you get back home. You're to bunk with John Noseworthy from down north."

Sailor was making himself acquainted with some of the crew. He sniffed at duffel bags and nosed at boots and gloves. He seemed quite at home on the *Polar Star*. He probably remembered the *Thaddeus* of his puppy days.

Before the captain could turn away, a young boy hurried across the gangway and seized him by the arm. He was the one who had spoken to Tom at the store window.

"Captain, sir, you got a ticket for me aboard your ship?" he asked breathlessly.

"Sorry, me lad," said Captain Wight. "We've got no berth for boys your age. This is a man's ship."

The boy still clung to his arm. "Please, sir," he entreated, "I'm near thirteen years old. I'll work hard and I don't need much to eat."

"Run along, me boy," ordered the captain in a kindly voice. "Go home for another four years. Then come back and see me about a berth."

The boy lowered his blue eyes. He slowly released the captain's arm and turned back to the gangway. He stopped a moment to stare at Sailor enviously, then went ashore with his shoulders bowed in disappointment.

The *Polar Star's* whistle screamed across the harbor and echoed from the snow-sheeted hills. Cheery cries of goodwill from the wharves and nearby ships crackled through the sharp air. The ship's propeller thrashed like a whale's tail, and the

16

hawsers jerked loose like giant snakes. Slowly the ship backed into the loose ice of the harbor.

The vessel was an anthill of activity. Men crowded the rails and the rigging. From every foothold a figure waved and shouted. Sailor was up on the bridge with Captain Wight. The strong master bawled orders in a voice that carried like a fog-horn. "Hard aport! Steeay!"

Black smoke rose from the ship's funnel and melted into the murky mist over the town. The old steamer slowly turned and pointed her bowsprit toward the open sea.

The cannon boomed on the Battery side, and from the heights of the Narrows guarding the entrance of the harbor a sprinkling of St. Johnsmen waved caps and handkerchiefs. Then the *Polar Star* entered the ice outside and headed for the Northeast, following a dark narrow lead of water.

Sailor left the captain to make his own inspection of the vessel. He first made it his business to find the galley.

"Sure and it's the skipper's big dog going to sea with the rest of us old sea dogs," exclaimed one of the cooks. He hacked off a chunk of meat from a frozen slab and gave it to him.

Sailor carried the chunk out on deck, then lay down to gnaw at it. A man shouldering a basket of coal fell over him, scattering the coal all over the deck. He rose with an oath and would have banged Sailor with the empty basket if he hadn't been stopped by another crewman carrying a kettle of hot water.

"Hold it!" he warned. "That's the captain's dog."

In his frustration the clumsy one began to thrash the well-meaning man with the empty basket. The other threw the kettle

at him. Before they could take to their fists, three companions halted the fight.

"Save it for the swiles, ye puckaloons," cried John Noseworthy. He was a mighty Northman with a barrel chest and limbs like hawser posts. His handsome sealskin boots were almost as large as gunny sacks.

Sailor picked up his frozen chunk and went down to the main cabin below decks. It was a drafty room with smaller cabin doors opening on two sides. A black stove warmed one end. A barometer hung on the opposite wall. In the middle of the big cabin was a table covered with oilcloth. It was flanked by a lumpy leather chair and three benches.

The dog crawled under the table and settled on the linoleum to finish his meat in peace. He chewed up frozen mouthfuls, then took a nap. When he awakened, he was partially curtained by the edges of a white tablecloth. And the cuffs of loose trousers

ending in a remarkable pair of shoes were moving before Sailor's nose. The toes of the shoes turned up like the forerunners of Tom Boggan's sled, and the legs themselves moved with a stiltlike stiffness.

Sailor slowly crawled from under the table with his great black head raised. It met that of a scraggy little man with drooping walrus whiskers and popped brown eyes.

The eyes popped out even farther. The whiskers parted to emit a sirenlike screech. The tray in the man's twiggy fingers dropped to the floor and teacups shattered into pieces.

"Bear! Bear!" shouted the little man, racing away with odd, jerky steps. "Bear in the cabin!" his voice screeched down the passageway above the whine of the wireless operation.

There were shouts from that direction and much laughter. Sailor stood with the roots of his ears strained, trying to understand the commotion.

Soon the steward returned in embarrassment. "Foggy" Fogwill had learned his error. The banter was good-natured because he was a highly respected man aboard. Wasn't he one of the survivors of the *Newfoundland* tragedy? Fifty-six hours out on the ice in a blizzard had frozen his toes off. This accounted for the upright tilt of his shoes—there was nothing to hold them down in front.

Foggy brought broom and pan and began sweeping up the litter of crockery.

"Better broken cups than a broken propellor," he said to Sailor with good humor, "and all the less to wash."

Supper tea was served later with Captain Wight sitting on the

20

leather chair at the head of the table, surrounded by his officers and master watches. The dim light from the lamp swinging overhead gave Sailor's dark coat a bronze cast.

Foggy brought in a tray of covered pans and more crockery. "Plenty for all," he said cheerily, "but some'll have to share teacups till I can steal more from the crew's pantry."

The captain gave Sailor a formal introduction. "This big fellow is Sailor," he said. "He'll work as hard as any man pulling the sculps over the ice, complain less, and ask no share in the profits. And he'll give no favor to anyone."

Later the table was cleared and Captain Wight sat with his blue chart, plotting the course. He was busy with an important calculation when the boatswain came in unceremoniously dragging a young boy by the collar of his jacket.

"Stowaway, sir," he reported. "Found the little jackeen behind that sled stowed on deck."

Captain Wight glowered at the ragamuffin with the familiar blue eyes and yellow hair under the big cap. He rose from the chair to his full height to glower the better.

"Didn't I tell you to go home for four years?" he roared.

The boy was frightened, but he pretended bravery as he faced the angry shipmaster.

"I wanted to go sealing worse than anything, sir," he answered in a steady voice. "I couldn't find no other way to do it."

Captain Wight banged his lumpy fist on the table. "And how can you be a sealer if you don't know how to obey orders?" he demanded.

"I'll obey any order but go back," maintained the boy.

The captain addressed himself to the boatswain. "Throw him overboard!" he commanded.

The boatswain grinned broadly as his hands clamped the boy's shoulders like cant hooks.

A hint of fear crossed the boy's face. "I can't swim, sir," he said.

"He can't swim," the captain repeated to the boatswain. "So we'll wait until we get off Labrador and set him adrift on an ice pan." He fastened the boy with piercing eyes. "What's your name?"

"Jamie, sir," answered the stowaway. "James Piercey."

"Where are you from?"

"They say my father's people came from the island of Jersey, sir. That's what they say."

"I'm not asking where your ancestors stowed away from," snapped the captain. "Where do you belong?"

"I've been with different families, but now I'm with the Critches."

"Who are the Critches and where do they live?" asked the captain with dwindling patience.

"Mr. Critch has a fish wagon in St. John's, and Mrs. Critch is his wife. They've already got ten children, so Mr. Critch said one more didn't make any difference when they took me. Said he couldn't half the time tell which was the extra one."

"Where are your own parents?"

"My father drowned off the Banks, fishing. That's what they say."

"And your mother?"

"Mrs. Critch said she went off and got married again. She never did come back to get me."

"How long have you lived with these Critches?"

"Some years now, sir, until I ran off the other morning."

"My sympathy to them," said the captain. "Unlucky mortals who opened their home to a thankless boy who steals away with no fare-ye-well."

"But it's like Mr. Critch said," insisted the boy. "If one more don't matter, one less oughtn't either. And Dick's big enough now to help him and Meg with the fish wagon."

"Well, they'll have to know where you are for what little consolation it may give them," Captain Wight informed him. "I'll have our Marconi man send a wireless back to St. John's that you're aboard my ship."

"Thank you, Captain, sir. I guess they'll be wonderful surprised when they find out."

Captain Wight ordered the boatswain, "Take him down to the galley and feed his mouth, then send him to give the firemen a hand with anything they need."

As the pair started to leave the captain's manner changed. He put his hand gently on the boy's shoulder.

"It's going to be no easy voyage for you, me boy," he cautioned. "I know because I ran away from home to the sealing myself when I was nigh your age."

Later Captain Wight called for Tom Boggan.

"We've got a stowaway on board," he told him.

"Yes, I saw him, sir," said Tom. "I'm afraid what I said to him on the street encouraged him to hide aboard. I was telling him that the only way a boy can go sealing nowadays is by stowing away. I'm awfully sorry, sir."

"You only told him the truth," said the captain. "He'll need sleeping space. How about him sharing the bunk with you and John Noseworthy?"

"It's fine with me," agreed the young man. "That big Northman tries to take more than his share of it, so the boy will make a good dividing line between us."

III

The Seal Hunt

The *Polar Star* slowly nosed her way through open leads of water or butted ahead into solid ice. Great cracks sprang from her bow like black water snakes. The ice pans spun and grated against her stout sides. When the sea was heavy, the pans of ice rose and fell as if the north wind were shaking out its white carpet. Sometimes the ship was up on the crest of a great arctic mountain; then it would slide down into a deep valley between snowy peaks.

Sailor seemed to enjoy the cold ride, but Jamie Piercey shivered in his worn jacket.

Captain Wight noticed that his clothing was not sufficient.

"Come into my cabin, me boy," he ordered, "and I'll find you some warm wear. You look like a nogg-head in those rags."

"What's a nogg-head, sir?" inquired the boy.

"It's a skinny motherless seal with a raggedy coat and big eyes like you."

The captain walked ahead, his arms clasped behind his back, and Jamie followed.

In the captain's cabin Jamie's eyes took in what to their sight was the greatest luxury. A wooden bunk was neatly covered by a quilt pieced by Mrs. Wight's own hands. There was a desk, a comfortable armchair, and a hand basin set in a carved mahogany stand. But most remarkable of all were the shelves of books and the rack of telescopes, sextants, and other ship's instruments. Jamie's fingers itched to handle them, but he didn't dare. That did not keep his eyes from running over them.

"Do you need all them things to run a ship?" he asked.

"All of them, an able crew, and a mountain of coal," answered Captain Wight.

He opened his chest and, after some shuffling and indecision, pulled out a bright red guernsey sweater.

"Just the thing for you, lad," he said. "My Sarah knitted it, so the weave is warm and tight. Here, try it on for fit."

The boy took off his worn jacket and slipped into the sweater. The cuffs hung well below his fingertips, and the ribbed border almost reached his knees.

"Not cut to your jib exactly," acknowledged the captain. He turned the ends of the sleeves well up the boy's arms. "But just as well. You'll get double warmth on the lower arms and your stern will be protected."

"Nothing of Mr. Critch's ever fit me right either," said Jamie.

He was so proud of the guernsey that he didn't want to put the old jacket over it, but Captain Wight insisted on it.

"Every layer helps," he reminded the boy.

26

Jamie had little time to admire his new red guernsey. He felt that he was the busiest hand on the ship.

"Jamie-e-e!" one of the firemen would shout. "Make up a kettle of tea and bring it down to the engine room. They're sweated dry down there."

"Look alive, boy," the boatswain often bawled. "Shovel this slush off the decks."

"We've got a fair wind now," Captain Wight might call from the bridge. "Put up three staysails, and tell the boy to help. He can't learn about sails too young. Put on the spanker too."

"Anybody seen Jamie?" queried Foggy Fogwill three times a day. "I need somebody to dry dishes."

"Where's that little stoleaway?" one of the cooks was bound to ask. "We want him to fetch water from the tank."

Jamie thought that he must be the most important hand aboard the vessel.

"I'm sure showing them I can work like a man," he confided to Sailor. "They'll be glad they've got me along to help get seals. And I don't see what *you* would have done if I hadn't stole away." For it was another of the boy's chores to feed Sailor every evening and see that he always had water.

"He don't eat much for a dog his size," he confided to Foggy, "but I bet even a whale can't drink so much water. All I do is fill up his bucket, and you know how rusty and bracky that water is getting to be."

"It won't last much longer," said Foggy. "Then we'll hitch up to the ice and break off pinnacles to melt. They make the purest kind of water because there's so little salt in them."

But Jamie sometimes found time to loiter and talk on deck.

"When do we get to the seals?" he asked one of the firemen who was off duty. He was a brawny shock-headed young man whose mighty chest under the thin undershirt rose and fell like the sea. "Seems like we've put on enough sail and heaved enough coal and drunk enough tea to be there soon," continued the boy. "Seems like I can't wait another day to go on the ice after them."

The fireman looked at him sharply, then changed the subject. "See the flag on my arm?" he asked, calling attention to a tattoo. "Watch it wave." As he spoke he began flexing his muscle so that the flag truly did ripple as if it were cloth in the breeze.

"Cricky!" exclaimed Jamie. "I'd like to get one of them put on me when I get back to St. John's. But aren't you cold up here in those bare arms and nothing much on? I'm froze solid with Captain Wight's big guernsey under my jacket."

"Glorianna!" cried the fireman, waving the flag one more time. "It's so hot down in that engine room, it takes me half an hour on deck to cool off comfortable." He lifted the blackened sweat rag from his shoulder and rubbed off his coal-rusted forehead as if he were still suffering from the heat.

Jamie could understand. "Every time I bring something down there," he agreed, "I feel like a bag of duff dropped into the boiling pan."

Sailor came lumbering down the deck to join them. He rose on his hind legs with his forepaws against the railing, and his nose twitched.

28

"He don't mind the cold either," commented Jamie. "I tried to get him to sleep by our bunk, but he always spends the night up on deck. No wonder, when Tom Boggan snores and John Noseworthy talks in his sleep. Not that you can understand what he says most of the time."

"He won't sleep in the captain's cabin either," said the fireman, "and I can tell you we never see him down in the engine room."

The next day they passed a small patch of harp seals. Spring migration had brought them south from the Baffin waters to whelp their young whitecoats on the ice pans off Labrador. The men swarmed to the rails. It was like the leavetaking from St. John's. Only obedience to their strong captain and the stronger law that the season would not be open for a few more days seemed to keep them from leaping over the side.

The seals were oblivious of their close brush with death. The adults were sporting about like summer bathers on a beach. Scattered among them were the roly-poly white pups with their black eyes and noses. They made plaintive sounds like the crying of babies.

Jamie was even more excited than the men.

"Look at that old seal woggling all over the ice," he cried. "I bet he's telling the others we're here." He leaned far over the rail with his hands gripping the icy wood.

In their own excitement the men did not notice him. They too jabbered and pointed.

"Look at that ma seal," shouted the boy. "She's trying to push her baby down that hole. And her—"

His fingers slipped. He grabbed for a rope but missed it.

Headfirst he went over the side and dropped into the choppy water. Its hard coldness was like a blow of the north wind's fist. The black water closed over his head, and his old cap went floating away.

"Man overboard!" shouted the lookout in the barrel on the mast.

There was a tangle of confusion on deck. The seals were forgotten.

"The boy's in the blue drop," cried John Noseworthy.

"Man the starboard lifeboat," shouted the boatswain.

Suddenly there was a streak of black across the deck as Sailor made for the rail. He hurtled over it and dived into the ocean. When his black head came up, it was headed for the struggling boy.

"Man and dog overboard!" cried the lookout.

Meanwhile Captain Wight on the bridge had shouted orders to stop the ship. Her engines groaned and shuddered as they were put into reverse. The winches were already swinging a lifeboat over the side with Tom Boggan and John Noseworthy in it.

Confused and terrified as he was, Jamie could see the great paws coming toward him. He could hear the dog's heavy breathing. The boy thrashed his arms and legs to try to stay above the surface, but his struggles were futile. As the icy waves closed over his head again he felt a jerk at his collar and a soft, hairy nose against his neck. Up he came again with a steady haul at his jacket. He threw his arms around the dog's neck and clung like a barnacle.

Sailor could not decide which way to drag the boy to safety.

30

The sides of the ship were too high for a dog. Across the water the adult seals were madly scuttling down their bobbing holes or slipping into the water. Only the bawling whitecoats were left behind.

The dog started for an ice floe.

"Here, Sailor!" shouted Tom Boggan from the lifeboat which was now in the water. "Come here!"

Sailor swirled around and made for the lifeboat. When they reached it, Jamie stretched an arm to Tom. He was somersaulted over the side, choking and shivering.

As soon as the boy was safe in the boat, Sailor turned and began swimming away.

"Come back, Sailor!" shouted John. "You'll have to get into the boat."

The dog ignored him. He kept swimming until he reached Jamie's floating cap. He seized it in his jaws, then turned around. He swam straight to the boat.

John Noseworthy had upended Jamie and was giving him a shaking that made water run in trickles from his nose and mouth. Tom Boggan helped Sailor clamber over the side by grabbing fistfuls of his hair.

The winches raised the boat again and swung it over the deck. Jamie shivered and his teeth chattered as he took his cap from Sailor. Even Tom and John Noseworthy were wet, but Sailor, after one good shake of his coat, looked dry as the piles of coal on deck. He jumped out of the lifeboat, then sat down on the deck with his red tongue hanging out. He had followed the best tradition of his breed; he had saved a human being from drowning. He had even saved the boy's cap.

31

Captain Wight descended from the bridge. He proudly patted Sailor. "You're a real Newfoundland dog," he said in compliment. "A brave hero and a credit to the crown colony."

Then he clasped his hands behind his back and glared at the shivering Jamie. "And you're a clumsy little sprat not worth saving," he roared. "I should have thrown you overboard long ago."

Jamie stood with bowed head, rivulets of water running from his clothing and making puddles on the deck. He twirled the sopping cap in his hands.

"I'm wonderful sorry, sir," he humbly declared. "I'll never do it again."

Captain Wight beckoned to Tom. "Take him below and strip off his wet clothes," he ordered. "Tell Foggy to wrap him in my blanket. John, you go with them, and all of you drink some hot tea."

Sailor followed them.

All the rest of the day he dogged Jamie's feet. And when the boy went anywhere near the rails, Sailor grabbed the edge of his jacket and pulled him back.

"He's worried about me," said Jamie. "I guess he'll sure worry plenty when I go out on the ice after the seals."

But Jamie was in for a bitter disappointment that evening. The men down 'tweendecks were in high spirits when he joined them. Only their gaiety livened the dreary surroundings. The light was dim, the overhead so low that a tall man like John Noseworthy couldn't stand straight, and the two cracked stoves sitting in pans of deep ashes gave less warmth than the men's bodies. Some were sprawled on their bunks smoking and talking. Others were sharpening their gaff points or splicing rope. They were so happy that some of them began to sing at their work.

> The little Kite, she hove in sight
> With all her colors flying—
> The women busy starching shirts
> With pans of beefsteak frying.

Two of the men began beating the time on their food tins. More of them joined the chorus.

33

It seemed to be the little Kite.
She never missed her patches.
She struck them on the twenty-fifth
And filled her to the hatches.

"I hope we get enough seals to fill us to the hatches," said Jamie. "But where do I get my gaff so I can sharpen the point?"

A Placentia Bay man who was mending his boots gave Jamie a sympathetic look. "Me poor lad," he said, "you're not going to do any swiling."

"But that's why I came," said Jamie. "And I've been working hard to show everybody I'm able to do a man's work."

"It's a matter of shares, me lad," continued the man. "If you went on the ice and killed just one seal, you'd have the right to demand a share of the profits."

"But I won't," declared Jamie. "I promise I won't ask no share. You believe me, don't you?" He addressed himself to those nearby. "I double promise not to ask a share. All I want is to be a seal hunter."

The Placentia Bay man only shook his head and went on with his mending.

Jamie could not say another word. He stumbled out of the 'tweendecks and up the companion ladder. He hid behind a nest of lifeboats as alone as he could get.

After all his trouble to get aboard a sealer! He had gone from ship to ship asking for a berth, and at each one he had been turned away with the curt explanation that there was no place for a boy. Then he had regained hope when the friendly young man with the big dog had told him about stowaways.

34

And he had been successful at hiding on the deck of the *Polar Star*. Hadn't he shown them that even though he was a boy, he could do a man's work? It often seemed as if he were doing the work of four men. U. S. 1462759

Jamie buried his face in his hands, and his shoulders shook with sobs. Suddenly a moist hairy object brushed his neck. It was Sailor's blunt muzzle. He seemed to be trying to comfort the boy.

Jamie put his arm around the dog's shaggy neck and pressed his cheek against the white spot on his chest. Then he picked up a handful of slush from the waterway and rubbed it across his eyes.

"They can't keep me young forever," he told the dog. "I'll come back to the sealing every spring, and they'll have to put a gaff in my hand after a while."

As the *Polar Star* rammed her way ever northward, the patches of seals became more frequent and larger. The men's excitement grew, and Jamie could not help feeling some of it even if his experiences were to be secondhand.

On the evening before opening day for hunting, the men were gathered in the murky 'tweendecks putting last-minute touches to tools and clothing. The boy sat on the edge of a bunk watching and listening.

"Tomorrow we'll be in the fat for fair," declared John Noseworthy in his raw husky voice, "and a fine garagee 'twill be."

"Is it dangerous to hunt seals?" asked Jamie.

"There's no danger from the young ones," put in the Placentia Bay man, "and the old ones usually run away, but you never can tell when some old swile will stick her head up out of the bobbing hole and nip you good in the seat of the pants while you're sculping her pup."

"What's the bobbing hole?" asked the boy.

"You've seen all those holes over the ice pans," he was informed. "The swiles make them to come up to their pups. Queer thing! Those big swiles can swim a hundred miles away, but they'll always come up just the right bobbing hole."

Next morning dawn came over the eastern horizon, turning the white floes to pink. The ice-coated masts and rigging glittered as if the vessel were made of glass. The men gulped their heavy breakfast of salt meat, bread, and jam without seeming to taste a mouthful. They scalded their throats with strong tea.

The lookout in the barrel was combing the ice with his spyglass. Below him clustered men armed with gaff poles and coils of rope—and a boy and a dog. Everyone was on the knife edge of excitement.

"The swiles are too scattered yet," said one of the veterans. "The captain's having us wait until we hit the big patches."

Finally the electrifying cry came from the barrelman, "Big patch of whitecoats ahead!"

The ship was conned alongside a sheet of ice as large as a snow-covered meadow.

"Overboard, me boys!" shouted Captain Wight. "Jump into the fat! It's free-for-all and the old boy take the hindmost."

There was a scramble with no regard for gangs or master watches as there would be on later rallies. Like ants they swarmed over the sidesticks and down the ropes.

36

"Go with them, Sailor," ordered the captain in his foghorn voice. "You can help tow the sculps to the marker."

Sailor started after the men. But he soon turned and looked back at Jamie. He whined, then returned to him. He nipped at the boy's jacket.

"He has to stay aboard," cried the captain. "Go with the men, Sailor."

The dog looked up at him. He looked at the figures jumping over the side. He sat down at Jamie's feet.

The boy gave him a shove. "Go do what the captain says," he ordered.

But Sailor wouldn't obey.

"Then let him stay," decided the captain. "I'll have him court-martialed for mutiny later." There was a wide grin above his beard.

The hunters raced toward the bawling whitecoats and their nimble parents, who were ducking down bobbing holes. Swiftly they dispatched whitecoat after whitecoat with a quick hard blow on the snout. Almost as swiftly they rolled each plump body over and shucked off the pelt with its lining of fat. These sculps were then fastened to ropes and pulled into one big pile. "Scoting the tow" John Noseworthy called it.

Each man tried to get as many as possible but not because they would be credited to him. The hunters would share equally in the gains, and the captain and members of the crew would be given a percentage. But the harder a man worked, the more profit there would be for everyone.

Captain Wight left the bridge and joined Jamie at the railing.

37

He had forgiven him for falling overboard. "It's a good start, me boy," he said, "and before we finish the voyage, we should be down to the gunwales with the weight of the sculps."

Jamie was silent for a while, watching the black figures running over the ice like ants over sugar. He noticed the thin red lines that spread behind them as they dragged their sculps to the marker. Somehow he had imagined seal hunting to be more valorous and the struggle more evenly matched.

He said, "It don't seem right, sir, killing the little creatures that don't even fight back."

Captain Wight turned to him. "But those little creatures grow into big seals," he pointed out, "and it is reckoned that there are already over two million of them in these waters. Have you gone to school any?"

"Sometimes Mrs. Critch makes Meg and me go," answered the boy. "We're about the same age, and Meg seems more like my real kin than the others."

"Since you go to school sometimes, let's see how good you are at sums," suggested the captain. "Now figure that each seal eats one codfish a day, me boy. How many fish is that in only one day?"

"Two million. That's easy. I'm good at sums in school. But I'm only in the third reader. Meg's in the fourth."

"All right," continued the captain. "Now, how many fish does that add up to in a year?"

"That's harder," acknowledged Jamie. "Nobody ever bought that many fish from us. I'd need paper and pencil."

Captain Wight readily produced an old envelope and the stub of a pencil from his pocket.

Jamie held the paper against the railing. "How many days has a year got?" he asked.

"Three hundred and sixty-five and every leap year one day more."

Jamie licked the point of the pencil, then scowled as he slowly began the ordeal of multiplication. "Seven hundred and thirty million!" he exclaimed with a low whistle. "Maybe I better check it over."

"No need," the captain assured him. "Now you can easily see how many fish a year are being taken from the fishermen's nets by the seals—not even counting leap years."

Jamie nodded. "Mr. Critch wouldn't have nothing to sell if it wasn't for the fish."

The captain's glove squeezed the railing. "It's a hard life we live in this north land, Jamie," he said. "It's a hard life in a hard land. So we have to be hard too if we want to survive."

"Yes, sir," said Jamie. "I understand."

IV

The Storm

After the first free-for-all on the ice, the rallies were organized and tightly disciplined. The master watches lined their men up on deck and checked their equipment. One group after another climbed the railing.

"Fore starboard watch over," bawled Captain Wight.

The men immediately crawled over the sidesticks and slid down the ropes. These stalwart hunters would cover many miles and kill many seals. But the compass in each master watch's pocket would unerringly lead them back, towing their ropes of sculps, to the exact spot where the ship would pick them up many hours later.

The *Polar Star* slowly inched ahead until the captain ordered, "Aft starboard watch over," and another group, including Tom Boggan, scrambled to the ice.

So it went until all the hunters had left the ship. But again

Sailor refused to leave since Jamie wasn't going. He seemed to have assumed responsibility for the boy's safety.

Captain Wight scanned the skies and consulted his barometer for any suspicion of bad weather in the offing. At the hint of an approaching storm he would blow the siren as a signal for the distant men to return immediately to the pickup points. Too many hunters had lost their lives in sudden blizzards that swept down from the arctic and trapped them on the ice.

One day when the men were out, Captain Wight had his own compass brought to him. As he set it on the table, Sailor came wandering in.

"Where's Jamie Piercey?" he asked the dog. "Go fetch Jamie to me."

Sailor turned and set off on the quest because he knew very well that the boy was safe 'tweendecks.

"Bring me a cup of hot tea, Foggy," shouted the captain toward the pantry. "I've some talking to do."

It was not long before Sailor returned, leading Jamie by a mouthful of his jacket.

"I don't know what's the matter with him, sir," said the boy "but he's been pulling at me like I was about to fall overboard."

"I told him to bring you," said the captain in a matter-of-fact voice. "He was only carrying out my order. I want to give you a lesson while my compass is here. No use in setting you ashore as stupid as when you boarded my ship."

"I've learned a lot already," said Jamie.

"Then you'll learn to box the compass today," the captain informed him.

The boy did not object to this kind of a lesson. He squeezed in front of the captain and looked at the compass in its scrolled brass setting. It was a magic thing to him, and the way its needle unwaveringly pointed to the magnetic north seemed pure witchcraft.

Foggy brought in the tea and a plate of richly buttered toast to accompany it. The boy's eyes devoured the toast, so the captain set it in front of him.

"Help yourself, me boy," he said. Captain Wight took a gulp of the tea, then set the cup on the edge of the table. "See here," he told Jamie, "the compass has thirty-two points. Beginning at the top we have north, then north by east, north-northeast, northeast by north . . ."

Jamie's eyes circled the compass clockwise along with the

44

captain's horny finger as the warm butter dribbled down his chin.

That was only the beginning. There was southeast by south and southwest by south and all the combinations possible. And most important, there was the lubber's line on the rim which marked the ship's bow and the course.

"There are wonderful many ways to go, aren't there, sir." Jamie said with awe, brushing the butter off his chin with the sleeve of his jacket.

"And one of them you don't want to go," replied Captain Wight. "That's straight down to the bottom." He added, "But I don't like the way the barometer has been falling. I'd better order the ship back for the men. You stay here and watch the needle. Even when the ship turns, it will keep pointing to the north."

Jamie obeyed, eating the last slice of toast while his eyes were glued to the compass. As the captain had said, even as the ship turned it was true to the magnetic north, but the lubber's line swung around.

Later Captain Wight briskly returned to the cabin. "They'd better not be empty-handed; or I'll leave them out on the ice all night."

Jamie was shocked by this threat until he remembered that the captain had ordered him thrown overboard but hadn't meant a word of it.

Captain Wight lifted the cup on the table and took a swallow of the black tea. He set it down quickly. "It's cold as the pinnacle it came from," he complained. Then he said to the boy, "I'll show you another smart trick Sailor can do." Jamie waited for a new wonder.

The captain addressed the dog. "You look thirsty, Sailor. You may help yourself to the tea now."

The dog looked at the captain uncertainly, then wagged his tail. He lifted his muzzle to the edge of the table, balanced the big cup on his lower jaw, then slowly walked to a corner. He set the cup down as carefully as he had picked it up. He began to lap the tea fastidiously with his big tongue.

"Little crackies only understand certain words," explained the captain, "but a Newfoundland understands whole sentences."

"I sure wish I had a big dog like him," said Jamie enviously.

"Sailor surely has taken to you," admitted the captain, "and if you had a home of your own, I'd give him to you. I can't take him back with me because there's a law against dogs in my cove. Sailor's been banished."

Jamie began to tremble with excitement and his eyes lit up.

"Oh, would you please let me have him, sir?" he begged. "The Critches won't mind if I bring him back. Like Mr. Critch said, one more don't matter. There's plenty of fish to eat and he could sleep in the stable with Daisy. That's the horse."

Captain Wight dashed his hopes.

"I'm sorry, boy, but it wouldn't be fair to the Critches or to Sailor. Sounds to me like they're overcrowded already."

Jamie's eyes blurred and he could feel his Adam's apple swelling in his throat. It was the second big disappointment of the trip. Becoming Sailor's master would have erased the first one. He fought back the tears gathering behind his eyelids. He must show the captain that he was a man even if he wasn't allowed a part in the hunt.

"I know how hard it will be to give him up, sir," he said. He really did know because he too was having to give up the dog since he had no place of his own for him.

The men had had a successful day on the ice. They were gathered around great piles of sculps as the *Polar Star* came to get them. They were stamping their feet and slapping their arms against their sides. John Noseworthy stood with his boots deep in the fat of a sculp to keep his feet warm. The ship's winches swung out and hoisted one ropeful of sculps after another. The crew on deck cheered the cold, weary hunters.

The *Polar Star* sailed unerringly down one lead of water after another to pick up the watches at the scattered points, as if she had the instinct of an adult seal to reach the right bobbing hole.

"Come aboard, all hands," the captain ordered the last group. "There's a storm brewing."

"It do look knobbly to the north," stated John Noseworthy.

The men seemed to lose their weariness. They climbed up the ropes and over the sidesticks like agile monkeys. They dug their gaffs into the scarred railing and leaped onto the deck.

Their work was not finished yet. The sculps had to be counted, stowed below, and iced down to prevent spoilage.

"One, two, three, four . . ." counted a voice deep in the hold. ". . . eighteen, nineteen, twenty."

"Score," shouted the master watch at the open hatch above as he cut a notch in his tally stick.

Jamie was drafted to help, and it seemed to him that he needed another pair of hands and feet. He helped carry baskets of ice to the hatch until he felt as if his back was broken and his hands frozen.

"Look alive, me boys," the captain ordered. "The storm's coming fast. Lucky everybody is aboard."

That evening despite the gathering tempest, the greasy, reeking men gathered 'tweendecks in high fettle. Again there was fresh meat—the flippers they had cut from the seal sculps. They fried them with onions on the bare top of the stove. John Noseworthy added more to those he had already strung on a short piece of rope.

"I'm scoting them home to my family," he explained. "They don't get much meat."

Jamie was surprised to learn that John had a family. He seemed so complete by himself.

"Do you have any boys my size?" he asked.

"All girls—three of them," answered John proudly. "The finest crew of girls on Notre Dame Bay."

It seemed even more unfitting that John Noseworthy's family should be made up of girls. It wasn't until some time later Jamie learned from Foggy that John's wife was an Eskimo woman from Labrador, and that she and the girls had chewed the sealskin of his handsome boots to make them soft and pliable.

Clouds of smoke from the frying flippers mingled with the gray fog from the men's pipes. The hunters ate ravenously, then lounged on their bunks or performed various personal jobs as they talked about the day's hunt. Despite Jamie's feelings about the seal pups, the men's stories filled him with envy.

As had been predicted by the barometer, the wind began to lash the masts and rigging. It thrashed the sea into a fury,

48

and the ship rose and fell in the icy maelstrom. Great ice pans thudded against her beams. Her timbers groaned and shivered. Sleet mixed with snow blinded the lookout.

"'Tis airsome weather," declared John Noseworthy.

"It was such a storm wrecked the schooners in 1885," reminisced a man with a broken nose, taking the pipe from his mouth.

"Were they sealing ships?" inquired Jamie.

"No, they carried fishermen and their families who had spent the summer working on the Labrador coast. All loaded they were and ready to come home when the gale struck. They were blown aground on the rocks, and almost all aboard were drowned. When it storms hard now, you can sometimes hear the moans and cries of those poor lost ones."

Jamie's face paled. "Maybe it's just the noise of the wind," he said. The wind outside had a ghostly wail.

The crook-nosed man glared at him. "If you ever hear them," he said, "you'll be able to tell their screams from the screech of the wind."

"I've seen a ghost ship myself," said one of the men braced in the bunk by his legs and arms. "At midnight it was, and I saw her off the coast down north. She was in full sail and white as an iceberg."

"Maybe it *was* a berg," suggested Jamie.

"How could a ghost ship look like a berg?" asked the storyteller.

"That berg we saw a couple days ago," insisted Jamie, "I thought it looked just like a big ship."

The man snorted scornfully.

Then Tom Boggan was reminded of the ghostly apparition that had appeared to his uncle when he was driving home late one night.

"My aunt knew something was wrong when she opened the door," he recounted. "White as your ghost ship he was. Then he told her that a headless heifer had suddenly appeared and blocked the road."

"How did he know it was a heifer," Jamie broke in, "if it didn't have a head?"

Tom frowned at him. "Then my uncle took to his bed and lay there for a month. And the horse lay down in her stall for a whole month. She had to be dragged in a canvas to the pasture."

"Who dragged her there if your uncle couldn't get out of bed?" asked Jamie.

Now all of the men turned on him.

"He's a little heathen," declared the man with the broken nose. "He doesn't believe in the hereafter."

"He will when the flimes of fire begin swindging him," pronounced John Noseworthy.

"Oh, yes, I do," protested Jamie. "Mrs. Critch always made us older ones go to church on Sunday. She couldn't go because of the baby—whichever one it was."

A great blow staggered the ship for a few moments as it was battered against rafted ice. The north wind screamed with fury.

Jamie lay awake long after his comrades had fallen asleep. He was sure that he could hear the moans and cries of the drowned fisherfolk in the wind that blew through the rigging above.

50

The rolling of the ship threw John Noseworthy and Tom Boggan against him in turn. Sometimes he was squeezed between them like a skiff anchored between schooners.

"To the lifeboats, me byes," shouted John Noseworthy in his sleep. "She's sinking fast." At that one of his great legs came down on Jamie like a plunging masthead.

Jamie decided that if John was going to have nightmares, he would be more comfortable on the hard floor. He crawled over the snoring Tom and reached one foot to the floor. It came down on something soft and furry. There was a sudden yip. It came from Sailor. The dog had come to keep watch over the boy.

Jamie curled up between the dog's paws. Sailor's nearness filled him with warmth and a feeling of security.

The storm raged for two days, so there was no seal hunting. Men waded through water on the decks and returned with bruised shanks and wrenched arms. The captain's eyes grew hollow and bloodshot for want of sleep, and his voice hoarsened.

Jamie came upon Foggy on his knees in the pantry with his face buried in his dry, bony fingers.

"What's the matter?" asked Jamie. "What are you doing?"

"Haven't you ever seen a man pray on a weekday?" asked Foggy.

"God does seem close here with the ice ready to smash our ship and the water waiting to gulp us," observed Jamie.

The little man pulled himself to his stubby feet. "He's the needle on that compass you were studying, me lad," he said. "He brought me off the ice safe."

51

"But why did He save you and not the others?" asked Jamie.

Foggy looked bewildered by the question. "I don't rightly know," he finally admitted. "I think maybe He saved me because I believed He would."

V

Holiday

"Northwest by north, north-northwest, north by west . . ." Jamie finished counting off the points of the compass to the captain's satisfaction.

"That's good, me lad," he told the boy. "We'll make a sailor-man of you yet."

"It's a seal hunter I want to be, sir," Jamie corrected him. He was getting over his first squeamishness about the killings.

"Of course you do," Captain Wight assured him. "You've been a good boy, so I'm going to give you a treat. Tomorrow you get to go out on the ice with any of the others that want to go."

Excitement boiled in Jamie. "You mean I'll get a gaff and sculping knife and rope?" he asked.

Captain Wight gave him a stern look. "Have you forgotten that tomorrow is the Lord's Day again?" he asked severely. "You know there is no hunting on Sunday. Even the fires for the boilers below will be banked tonight."

Jamie's hope was like a chunk of ice dropped on the deck. He swallowed hard. To hide his disappointment he bent his head over the compass. Then he remembered to say, "Thank you, sir. Thank you very much."

"The firemen like to get out on the ice and lark around," said the captain. "You can pack a nunny bag and make a picnic of it. Come with me and I'll give you something to put in it."

Jamie followed him through the door into his cabin.

Captain Wight slowly unlocked a drawer in his desk. "I hide my real treasures in here," he told the boy. Then from the drawer he pulled a golden orange and handed it to Jamie. The boy rolled it around in his hands with awe.

"It looks like the sun for fair," he said. He examined his pockets to find one that had no hole, then tucked it in there.

"Now don't be telling anybody where you got it," said the captain in a voice as conspiratorial as if he were dealing in smuggled goods, "or they'll all be hinting around for some."

"Oh, no, sir," promised Jamie.

As he turned to go the captain called him back. "No hurry," he said. "There's nothing waiting more important than what I want to talk to you about. Sit down on the bunk there and make yourself comfortable."

Jamie slowly did so, trying not to let his full weight down to dent the smooth surface of Mrs. Wight's quilt.

"I never sat in anything so softish," he said. "It's like sitting in mush."

54

"I never get so used to soft things that I turn my nose up at the hard deck of a ship," boasted Captain Wight.

"No, sir. I can see that."

The captain drew his armchair closer to the bunk and seated himself. He leaned forward, stroking his beard. "Sailor has really taken to you," he began, "and so have I. You're a hardworking, willing little sprat."

"They make me be, sir," answered Jamie modestly.

"Now, how would you like to be my boy?" asked the captain. "How would you fancy going home with Sailor and me after the voyage is over and letting my wife and me raise you? Seems to me the Critches have more than their share of children, and Sarah and I never had the young ones we wanted."

Jamie let his full weight down on the quilt and looked at the captain in amazement. It was as if he were listening to one of the supernatural tales told 'tweendecks.

"You mean it, sir?" he asked unbelievingly. "You mean you'll take me with you and Sailor, and I'll get to keep the guernsey?"

"Of course I mean it," snapped Captain Wight. "Isn't my word any good on my own ship?"

"Oh, yes, sir," replied the boy. He added doubtfully, "But that first day—you said you were going to set me adrift on the ice once we got off Labrador."

The captain squirmed slightly in his chair. "You know that was a joke," he explained.

"Maybe you're joking now."

Captain Wight rose to his feet impatiently. "Be cripes!" he exclaimed irritably. "Do you want to be my boy or don't you?"

55

"Cricky and I do, sir," answered Jamie. "I want it wonderful bad. It's just hard to get used to it so sudden."

"You won't get used to it suddenly," the captain assured him. "You'll go on working around here like the unlawful stowaway you are. And you won't get any favors from me. And you won't get to hunt seals either. When we go back to Spanish Choice Cove, you'll go to school regularly like a proper boy. And when you're old enough, you'll go to sea with me every spring and learn to be a real sealer and maybe captain of your own ship someday."

"Thank you, sir," replied Jamie, trying to imagine this glowing future which was so beyond anything he had in mind the night he had hidden behind the sled. "And I'll still take good care of the guernsey."

"We'll see that Mrs. Wight fixes some proper clothes for you when we get back," interposed the captain. "And, mind you, this is all a secret between you and me—like the orange. I don't want anybody favoring you because of it. Now run along, boy. Don't be idling away your time here."

Jamie paused with one foot across the hatchway combing. "But what about Sailor?" he asked. "You said you couldn't keep him in your cove?"

The captain jerked at his beard with perplexity. "Get along, boy!" he repeated. "Don't bother me with impertinent questions. Go clean the scuppers. They must be chock-full of gurry by now."

Jamie moved with alacrity to do his bidding. His heart was so light, never had worked seemed so easy.

56

Sundays were always strangely quiet. Since even the ship's fires had been banked for the day of rest, the firemen could cool off and forget the baskets of coal. The *Polar Star* drifted easily in an ice-formed harbor of still water.

The rugged sealers neatened themselves as best they could for the church services. They were led by "Preacher" Cuft, as they called one of the crew because he wore the buckle of the Christian Lads organization on his belt.

Although water was usually at a premium, it was used in what seemed a lavish manner to Jamie. Especially as he had to carry most of it.

"Why do *I* have to work on Sunday?" he asked. "Nobody else does."

"Haven't you heard that cleanness is next to goodness?" asked the Placentia Bay man. "Carrying water on the Lord's Day is no work."

Jamie washed his own face and hands and considered himself properly groomed, until John Noseworthy grabbed him by one ear and led him back to the community basin. "You slindged your neck and ears, me little puckaloon," he accused in his sonorous voice, "and your hair is in a shocking fruz."

He obligingly used his own comb on Jamie's blond mop after the boy had obediently dabbed some water over his neck and ears.

"There now," said Preacher Cuft, standing by. "You look enough like a Christian to pass inspection."

First they sang hymns, and it mortified Jamie that his voice was changing and broke on some of the high notes.

57

Preacher Cuft gave a short sermon reminding them of how close they were to eternity in their little ship on the hostile sea, although they really did not need this reminder.

After reciting the Lord's Prayer, more or less in unison, a few men took turns bearing witness to what the Good Lord above had done for them.

"I was a sinner until He took me in hand," said an old man with sunken eyes, "and even if this ship sinks, my soul will be saved anyhow."

Foggy Fogwill's testimony was the most impressive, although the men knew it by heart. "Aye, and don't forget the souls of those lost on the *Newfoundland*," he reminded them again. "Seventy-seven of them froze to death, and if it wasn't for His help, I would have been number seventy-eight brought into St. John's with the bells tolling. He gave me my life, so I don't begrudge Him taking my toes," he ended.

The fervor of the simple men was caught by Jamie Piercey.

"I'm a sinner too," he bore witness. "I ran away from the Critches and sneaked aboard this ship. But He must have forgiven me because something wonderful has happened. I can't tell what it is because it's a secret between me and the captain."

All of the men nodded and some of them ejaculated "Amen" because they felt that just the chance to sail on a ship with Captain Wight was a fine thing.

"As fine a man as ever broke a cake of the world's bread," John Noseworthy often said of the captain.

There was more praying and singing. Then the service was ended. The men who had stood reverently with bowed heads now burst into boyish frolic. They wrestled and cuffed each

58

other like polar bear cubs. They packed nunny bags and pulled on caps and jackets as if they had never gone on ice before.

"Beat you over the side," cried Tom Boggan to John Noseworthy. "Beat you in a race to the nearest pinnacle."

"I'm going too," cried Jamie. "The captain said so. Wait for me and Sailor."

Even the firemen were going on the ice for the sport of it. They seized gaffs for a joke, and when Sailor appeared on deck, they advanced upon him as if he were a whitecoat. Then they dropped the gaffs and went racing to the railing and over the sidesticks to see who could reach the ice first. Jamie ran them a close race, although Sailor tried to hold him back.

While Jamie was wondering how to get Sailor down the ropes, the dog leaped over the railing and plunged into the water. He was not content to climb up on the ice until he had circled the *Polar Star*.

Captain Wight watched him paddle around the bow.

"If he hadn't been born a dog, he'd have been a seal," he declared to the boatswain. He shook his head ruefully. "Too bad he wasn't. Then he'd be welcome in Spanish Choice. Oh, woe, woe, woe! I wish I had a compass to lead me out of this problem. It keeps getting more complicated. With all the men on this ship, why did that dog have to choose a homeless little sprat for his master?"

The men raced across the ice pans and leaped from floe to floe—these men who for the past six days had done the same in grinding labor to slaughter seals and haul back their sculps. But today was a carefree holiday. For Jamie and the firemen it was their first freedom from the tiresome decks.

The boy gleefully ran and slid where the ice was smooth. In rougher places he kicked at the pinnacles and threw chunks of ice for Sailor to chase.

In groups that became black dots on the white background the men wandered mile upon mile away from their ship until they no longer could see her masts on the horizon. But they were used to going great distances away during their rallies.

"Cricky, look at the big white mountain," cried Jamie, pointing ahead.

"That's a berg coming through the ice," said the fireman nearby. "Probably making a mile an hour. Come on boys! Let's hoof over and climb her."

They trudged on without feeling weariness or cold. The iceberg, like most, was high and sheer in back and sloped down to the surface of the ice cracking ahead of it. It shone white as frozen milk, with the sunlight dazzling on its peak.

The men, with their cleated boots, and Sailor with his sharp claws had little trouble making their way up the slippery incline. But Jamie kept falling and slipping back until two of the firemen came back and each took a hand. He was fairly dragged to the summit.

Once there, his feet found a flat shelf on which to stand. He surveyed the white desert that stretched endlessly in all directions. Then his eyes glistened as he pointed back. "Looky!" he shouted. "The *Polar Star!* We can see her again."

All eyes turned toward the vessel which looked as if it would fit in a man's pocket.

"Cricky!" exclaimed Jamie. "That shows the world really is

round like they told us in school. If it was flat, we could have seen the ship all along."

As they made their way downward the *Polar Star* and her masts slowly sank below the white horizon.

"My stomach's beginning to pick," said John Noseworthy.

"It's about time to eat," agreed one of the firemen, looking up at the sun, "and I've brought the wood. We'll make a fire here and boil up water for tea."

Jamie wondered where the wood was concealed, until the fireman pulled out a knife and began shaving the pole in his hand into a pile. He finished by chopping up the rest of the pole with a hatchet.

Jamie helped break off pinnacles of ice to melt in the kettle. Then he stood with his back to the fire, munching a handful of raisins that Tom Boggan had given him. He planned to save his orange for a couple of days so he could enjoy its smooth feel and bright color longer.

"Be jakers!" exclaimed the Placentia Bay man. "We've done a right foolie thing. Suppose that berg had started to roll while we were up there."

"Ho, ho!" laughed a fireman. "We'd have had our last look at the *Polar Star*."

"Do icebergs roll sometimes?" queried Jamie.

"That they do," said the other. "The water around starts churning like a whirlpool and great swells rise up. Then over goes the berg with a shower of ice and water."

"And over goes us too," said John Noseworthy, slurping his tea.

They munched the usual dry oatmeal mixed with sugar, but today it had the flavor of a feast. Some of them, including Tom Boggan, had brought raw onions for lung power, but Jamie was happier just feeling the orange in his pocket.

On the walk back they came upon a small patch of seals, and the men began lamenting that they did not have their gaffs and that it was Sunday.

"But you'll get a close look of a live whiteycoat," Tom Boggan told Jamie. Tom felt like a seasoned "swiler" now.

As they closed in on the seals, John Noseworthy made sharp barking sounds and, with elbows close to his sides, flapped his hands like flippers. The adult seals growled back in alarm, then wriggled to the nearest bobbing holes and ducked down them. Only the little whitecoats were left helplessly behind. Their big brown eyes stared trustingly at the men. Otherwise they showed no more life than puffy pillows.

Sailor raced after the fleeing seals, then stood looking down a hole as if he were making ready to follow them below.

"Come back, you foolie dog," shouted the Placentia Bay man. "You go below and those swiles will have your sculp."

The dog paid no heed to him. He tightened his muscles for the dive.

"Come back here, Sailor," ordered Jamie with a captain's authority in his voice.

Sailor gave the hole a last look, then humbly returned to the boy.

A fireman lifted a seal pup while Sailor curiously sniffed at its scutters. "Here, boy," said the fireman to Jamie. "Here's another pet for you."

The boy took the plump furry cherub into his arms. The cuddly white coat was softer than any feathers. He stroked the pup and felt its tickly whiskers. Tears gathered in its dark eyes.

"Today may be Sunday," reasoned the fireman, "but there's no law against carrying your whiteycoat back to the ship and sculping him tomorrow. You've been wanting to kill seals."

"No, no!" cried Jamie in alarm. "I don't want to kill him. He's so soft and tame. Please let's leave him here for his mom."

The man laughed good-naturedly. "Going soft on the white-coats," he teased. "They do seem like pet kittens."

Jamie said nothing more. He hurried to the nearest bobbing hole. It was no larger than a barrelhead and was surrounded by ramparts of ice raised by the mother keeping the hole open. He set the pup close to it.

"Now come tomorrow, you scoot," he advised it. "I'm going back to the ship," he informed the men. "I'm getting froze. Come on, Sailor."

The buoyancy was gone from his steps as he hunched his shoulders and began plodding back to the ice-locked harbor where the *Polar Star* drifted with cold engines amid the slob ice beginning to thread around her.

He had been wondering how they would get Sailor back on board again. Would they lower a lifeboat for him?

When they reached the ship, he found that an easy and ingenious way had been contrived. Captain Wight had made a bellyband of canvas. Two men with ropes lowered it, Jamie fastened it under the dog, and Sailor was easily brought up to the railing.

VI

Jamie's Decision

Late that night Jamie knocked at the door of the captain's cabin. When it swung open, he was surprised to see him in a long flannel nightshirt. The men below merely took off their boots and jackets before going to bed.

"So you've had a taste of the ice, and you've come begging to go on the hunt tomorrow," barked Captain Wight. "My answer is still no."

"It's not that, sir," denied Jamie. "It's the other way around. I don't want to be a seal hunter after all. I don't want nothing to do with it. It seems mean to kill the whiteycoats when even their own moms run away without helping them."

"One day on the ice without even a killing, and you've turned mawky and qualmish," accused the captain. "Is that what you're trying to tell me?"

Jamie nodded miserably. "Seems like the seals have as much right to the fish as us ones," he said. "They have to eat too."

65

"Then the deal between us is off," roared Captain Wight. "I don't want to raise any namby-pamby boy to follow in my boots."

"Yes, sir," said Jamie unhappily. "I thought it would be that way, so I wanted to let you know real soon."

"I should have set you adrift on an ice pan after all," exploded the captain, "but I'll spare you to go back to St. John's to peddle fish on the streets the rest of your life."

"If you're mad at me, sir, I'll give you the guernsey back," offered Jamie.

"A flame of fire take the guernsey!" raged Captain Wight. "I gave it to you to keep."

He slammed the door in the boy's face.

Jamie, with head hanging and feet dragging, returned below. He wasn't just giving up the chance to go home with Captain Wight and be his boy. He was giving up Sailor too. He had failed the dog as well as the captain.

"But I couldn't kill one of those little tame whiteycoats," he tried to explain to Sailor. "I couldn't even if I wanted to. And to think how bad I wanted to when I first came aboard!"

Jamie did not have much time to gloom over the unfortunate change in his destiny. He was kept too busy.

When dawn came, turning the ice into opals and diamonds, it found the *Polar Star* locked fast in the ice. Although the fires had been started up the night before, the steam pressure was still low. She would not budge an inch.

"Easy astern!" shouted Captain Wight. "Now full speed ahead!"

The engine stuttered, but the ship did not move.

"Us are shocking pinched up," declared John Noseworthy.

The captain tried a new plan. "Get every man alive up on deck," he ordered his boatswain. "We'll try to rock her loose."

The boatswain bugled down one hatchway after another, "All hands on deck! All hands on deck to roll ship!"

They scrambled from every opening, Jamie and Sailor with them. The boy's face, caked with dust from helping to pass the coal, was as black as that of the dog. It was hard to recognize any of the shining faces that had been present at the Sunday morning service.

"Line up portside!" bawled the boatswain.

They did so, bringing their combined weight to throw the vessel off balance and thereby break loose from the ice. But no listing resulted. The *Polar Star* was tight as a toy ship in a bottle.

"Now run, boys, run!" cried the boatswain.

They ran to the other side of the deck, bringing the weight there. Back to portside they ran again, trying to rock the ship loose. Jamie was proud that he could keep up with them. Even Sailor raced back and forth in what must have seemed like some kind of game to him.

"Faster! Faster!" shouted the captain. "Roll her, me boys!"

The race back and forth grew more frantic. They ran as if they were chasing a herd of agile old seals.

When Jamie felt as if he had run all the way to the Labrador coast and couldn't last any longer, the captain called a halt.

"She hasn't budged an inch," he called. "Save your strength to blast her out."

Some of the sweating men were sent overboard with axes to

begin chopping trenches in the ice. The green metal containers of blasting powder were brought out, and two men began filling small cans with the powder and fastening them on long sticks.

Excitement mounted until the men themselves seemed ready to explode.

"With all that powder we're going blow her out good or us up high," declared the Placentia Bay man. "You'd better take the dog below, Jamie boy. There'll be a bang to crack your ears. And maybe the whole sea will come down on us, or we'll go right up into the sky."

Jamie pulled Sailor into a companionway as the men below thrust the long poles deeply into the trenches. He shut his eyes and put his fingers in his ears.

There was a tense moment of dead silence among the men while the flame on the oakum fizzed. Then a series of deafening explosions shattered the ice and shook the ship.

"Full speed ahead!" roared the captain.

The *Polar Star* seemed to be shaking with her own terror as she surged ahead, but she was freed from the ice. Her progress was slow because of the thickness of the frozen field before her.

Later the barrelman cried from his observation post, "Iceberg dead ahead!"

"Then we'll follow in its wake and get a pull through this heavy ice," said Captain Wight.

Jamie learned another trick of the men who sailed the sealing ships. Once they caught up with the slow-moving berg, following the lead left open in its wake, some of the men set ice claws in its stern.

68

"Now we'll go along easy as if a grumpus is towing us," John Noseworthy told Jamie. "Nothing can stop a berg."

"What's a grumpus?" asked Jamie.

"It's a whale," said the Placentia Bay man. "Haven't you ever heard of whales?"

Jamie had a frightening thought. "Suppose that berg begins to roll?" he asked with big eyes.

"If it do," predicted the Northman, "they won't need narn of we running deck to roll ship."

When they finally reached a wide lead of dark water going off to the left, the claws were pulled from the iceberg. Seal hunting was resumed again.

As the great piles of sculps were brought aboard, the keel of the *Polar Star* sank deeper and deeper into the sea. And as the piles of sculps grew, the piles of coal diminished.

Jamie found it harder to go about his duties, as his way was blocked by heaps of their ever-increasing cargo. The decks became slimy with blood and running fat. The stench permeated the passageways and made the smell of the fish in Mr. Critch's wagon seem rarest perfume in contrast.

"Well, me lucky boys," cried the captain jubilantly, "we've taken thirty-five thousand sculps aboard. Let's make it forty before we turn south. And work lively. The coal's getting low."

Before they reached this figure, some of the men were turned out of their bunks to make more room for the seal hides. Jamie's bedfellows dragged Tom Boggan's sleeping sack to the flat top of a pile of diminishing coal. The boy took to sleeping on the floor with Sailor. The dog kept him warm enough without blankets.

69

The whitecoats were growing older and losing their value, so more and more adult seals were joining the load of sculps. Rifles were issued to the best marksmen, Tom Boggan among them.

They began hunting the vicious hood seals. Unlike the harps, the hood parents would defend their pups to the death.

The men returned from the hunts with faces blackened by gunpowder and with frostbitten hands.

"And there was me without a gun, and that old swile coming after me with his hood blown up like a spinnaker," recounted the Placentia Bay man. The male seal had a fleshy cap which he inflated to monstrous size when angered.

"It seems more fairsome hunting the hoods," stated Jamie.

The voyage would soon be over and he dreaded to think of its ending, for then he would have to part with Sailor.

72

VII

The Critches

In late April the *Polar Star* returned to St. John's with pennants flying and gunwales low in the water. It was almost as exciting as the leave-taking. But the scene was different. The snow and ice were gone, and the ridges above the harbor were beginning to turn green. It was still cold, and a haze of smoke screened the town.

Sirens screamed, and an English man-o-war in the harbor respectfully dipped her colors.

Again the men of the sealing vessel thronged the decks and hung from the ratlines. A less tidy group they were, if possible, than those who had sailed out to the icefields. Their faces and their clothing were black as the coal dust ground into the decks. Nearly every face was bearded, but the eyes staring out were brighter and filled with triumph.

Not Jamie's. This was no triumph for him. It was a bitter defeat. Soon he would have to part with Sailor and make his way back to the Critches.

The captain would be returning to his wife with the pride of having brought in such a large cargo of seals for his company. Tom Boggan would be going back with his own trap net. Even John Noseworthy would be bringing home a string of seal flippers to his wife and three girls.

But he, James Piercey, would be returning to the Critches empty-handed and disgraced. Perhaps Mr. Critch would throw him out for having run away.

Jamie dwelt on these thoughts while St. John's was giving them a royal welcome.

When the vessel had been secured to the wharf, the men's labor was not finished. The sculps must be unloaded and counted again. But Jamie was grateful for the work. It kept him on the *Polar Star* longer.

"And a fortune 'twill be, me lads," boasted the Placentia Bay man. "Nearly a hundred dollars apiece. Better than last year when I paid back my twelve-dollar crop and only had three dollars left for two months' work in the icefields."

Jamie was helping spread the sculps on the dock when Foggy brought him word that the captain wanted to see him in his cabin.

The boy found Captain Wight tidying his shaving gear and ready to change into a clean suit.

"I've had time to do some thinking since I got the ship back safely," he said. "And I've mostly been thinking it wouldn't be right to separate you and Sailor. You're the only one the dog has ever attached himself to."

Jamie's spirits leaped.

"Oh, thank you, sir," he cried. "I know that Sailor is such

74

a wonderful good dog that Mr. Critch won't mind having him. There'll always be plenty of leftover fish for him to eat."

"No, boy," said the captain. "We're going back on the original course I plotted for us. You'll come home with me. Maybe Tom Boggan can make a fisherman out of you anyway. It won't make you queasy to net fish, will it?"

Jamie's spirits rose as high as the masts of the *Polar Star*.

"No, indeed," he declared. "I'm used to dead fish. They don't seem human like seals."

"Not 'human,' Jamie," corrected the captain. "Even Sailor, intelligent as he is, isn't human."

"But he does seem like it," insisted Jamie. "Anyway I thank you for taking me when I won't be much good except to help Tom fish."

"Now, it's this way," said the captain, becoming methodical. "I'll have to be around here three days or so before I can get away. We'll drive out to these Critches now so I can talk with them. And perhaps it would be best for you to stay there until I'm ready to leave."

A sudden fear gripped Jamie. If the captain left him with the Critches, maybe he'd never return. Maybe he'd change his mind again or forget all about him.

"Please, sir," he said, "I don't want to go back to the Critches. I want to stay here with you."

Captain Wight glared at him. "There *are* Critches, aren't there?" he demanded. "It wasn't some cockaloo story you made up?"

"No, no," cried Jamie. "I want to tell them good-bye . . . and Meg. But—but—you'll really come back for me, won't you?

Maybe I could take Sailor there to stay with me," he added as a guarantee against the captain's failure to return.

"Do I look like an addlepate who forgets his responsibilities?" demanded Captain Wight. "And in case I am, Sailor will stay here to remind me about you."

Jamie was relieved. "I'm ready to go, sir," he said.

"No, you aren't," corrected the captain, pulling on his coat. "Look in the mirror. I can't tell your face and paws from Sailor's. Here! There's plenty of water left for you in the bowl. Wash up and don't forget your neck and ears. The clothes won't matter, because we're going home on a schooner."

Jamie obediently washed his hands, then leaned over the captain's white enamel bowl to wet his face. As he did so a strong hand fastened in his long hair and forced his face under. It was almost as bad as the ducking he had had off Labrador, only this water was warm and soapy.

When he thought that he was surely drowning, the iron fist yanked his head up. Jamie coughed and choked, his nose and eyes stinging from the soap. A towel was thrust into his hands.

"Now dry off and meet me at the forward gangway," said Captain Wight. "I've sent for a cab."

He left and Jamie stayed to finish drying himself. His restless eyes, ever interested when in the captain's cabin, saw that the sea chest was opened and already a few articles of clothing were neatly packed into it. He stripped off the red guernsey, proud that his jacket had protected it from dirt if not odor. He folded it to the precise measurements of the chest's width. He laid it carefully over the captain's personal effects. That

76

should help Captain Wight to remember. Then he put his old jacket on again and went hurrying down the passageway.

He saw the cab waiting near the gangway. A cobby horse was hitched to an open victoria, and a lantern-jawed driver was hunched in the high front seat. He showed no interest in the activities of the wharf.

Jamie had never ridden in a cab. He thought it would be like riding in a royal coach. He wondered what the Critches would think when they saw him returning in such style—probably that he had made his fortune in the seal fisheries.

While Captain Wight discussed some important matters with the boatswain, Jamie told his old shipmates good-bye.

"God bless you, my boy," said Foggy Fogwill, "and don't forget old Foggy."

A fireman wrestled him playfully, then pretended to aim his fist at Jamie's nose. "We didn't pull any sculps over the ice," he said as he pressed a twenty-cent piece into the boy's hand, "but we sure moved plenty of coal together."

"Fair weather to ye and snow to your heels," John Noseworthy wished him.

Almost everyone put a coin into his hand, until he felt that perhaps he had made a fortune on the trip.

Sailor's farewell for the three-day separation was more emotional. He howled dismally and tried to follow Jamie across the gangway. It took three men to hold him back.

"You have to stay here, Sailor," said the captain.

But the dog paid no attention to him. He howled louder and tried to force his way down the gangway.

The boy turned upon him sternly. "Stop that nonsense!" Jamie ordered. He pointed. "Sit there on the deck and wait until I come back."

Sailor stopped struggling with the men. When they released him, he dolefully sat down on his haunches. Only his great sad eyes followed Jamie.

"He feels the way I did when I thought I'd have to leave him for good," Jamie told the captain as they seated themselves side by side on the worn plush of the carriage seat.

"Where to, sir?" asked the cab driver in a voice that sounded as if it made no difference to him but might to the horse.

Captain Wight turned to Jamie. "What's their address?" he asked.

"It's on Clewe's Hill," answered the boy. "That's where the Critches live."

"Never heard of Clewe's Hill," commented the driver, although he clucked his horse to a start.

"It's way up," said Jamie. "It's northeast by east of here, I'd say."

The captain chuckled, but the cabbie remained glum.

"I should have brought my compass," said Captain Wight.

"You get up on Duckworth Street and I'll know my way from there," directed Jamie.

The ice and slush had disappeared from the streets, revealing cobblestones wet from a recent rain. The horse's hoofs clopped over them as the carriage went through the main streets of town. It seemed strange to Jamie to be back in civilization again.

"You turn left on King's Road, up this hill," he said to the driver after a while. "It's way up there."

78

Soon the boxy houses grew smaller and dingier, and the uncobbled roads steeper.

"It's the next corner," cried Jamie excitedly. "There's where Mr. Critch gets his tobacco."

The horse's hoofs moved slower and slower as she strained against the collar.

"Up that big hill and down the first alley," directed Jamie. "There's some of the Critches now."

A flock of children were hopping through a mud puddle like sparrows. A couple of them stopped playing to stare at the approaching rig.

Jamie waved. "Hey, Dick! Hullo, Edna and everybody."

A great twitter rose from the little flock.

"It's Jamie! It's Jamie come back."

They screeched and circled like hungry gulls.

The horse came to a slow stop, but not because her driver had halted her.

"I'm sorry, sir," the cabbie said to Captain Wight, "but you'll have to get out to lighten the load. And if you'll give a push from behind, it'll be a great help."

Jamie climbed out with alacrity. "We usually have to help Daisy pull the fish wagon up this hill," he said, "so I'm used to it."

"You see many seals, Jamie?" cried Dick. He was a boy a few years younger than James Piercey with a head of hair tousled by cowlicks.

"Did you bring any back?" cried a little girl who looked a year younger than Dick. In fact, all the children were stairsteps evenly spaced by a year.

"I'll tell you about it after a while," promised Jamie, putting

79

his hands to the spokes of the right rear wheel. Captain Wight obligingly tugged at those on the opposite side. In a flurry to help, the little Critches joined them in their labor. Slowly the wheels turned. The horse's hoofs moved forward and upward, her neck straining straight ahead.

"You turn in here," screeched the Critches in one breath.

"Ninety degrees to starboard," cried Jamie. Then, as they turned, "There's the barn."

Ahead of them and blocking the end of the alley was a stable with a horse's slouching rump visible in the gloom. In the shed at the side sagged a rickety wagon with the faded letters of J. CRITCH, FISHMONGER on the side curtain.

The fishmonger himself was coming from the stable to meet them and advise the cabbie how he could back up his rig to turn around. He was a man of uncertain age with a pale yellow mustache. When he opened his mouth to speak, there were gaps among his teeth.

"Jamie, boy," he cried. "It's good to see you back safe, you little rascal."

"This is my captain with me," said Jamie proudly. "He wants to talk to you about something."

"I'm Heber Wight, master of the *Polar Star*," the captain said.

"And I'm Jonathan Critch," answered the other, wiping his hands quickly on the gray apron tied around his waist. "Never thought to have this honor. I guess everybody in St. John's has heard of Captain Wight."

As the men shook hands a thin young girl came racing down the sagging outside stairway of the adjoining four-family house.

80

A snub nose and tangled red curls gave her a sprightly expression. She stumbled at the bottom but quickly regained her balance.

"Jamie," she cried. "It's really you and you wasn't drowned or nothing."

She ran to the boy and threw her arms around him. Jamie was embarrassed by her show of affection in front of Captain Wight. He roughly pushed her away.

"I'm too old for such mush now, Meg," he scolded her, "but I'm wonderful glad to see you again."

Then Mrs. Critch, the mother of this brood, leaned from a window above. She pushed back wisps of hair straggling over her forehead. She disappeared from the window to reappear at the door with a puckery new baby in her arms. She came down the stairs as if they had tired out her legs long ago.

"He's a new one, Jamie," she explained as she proudly held the baby toward him. "Born a couple weeks after you went. Little Willis."

Jamie gingerly touched the tip of his forefinger to the tiny red nose. "It didn't take you long to fill my place," he said reproachfully, but he grinned with an older brother's pride and embarrassment.

Mr. Critch and Captain Wight joined Mrs. Critch in solemn consultation about the something the captain had come to talk to them about.

The cab driver, his carriage reversed for the perilous descent of the hill, slumped for a quick catnap while he awaited his passenger's return.

The children knotted around Jamie.

"You've been gone a long time," said Meg. "Aren't you 'shamed to run away from us like this? Why didn't you take me along?"

"Girls can't go sealing, Meg. You know that."

"I could have cut off my hair and dressed up like a boy," she persisted.

"Did you kill many seals?" asked Dick impatiently.

"Oh, probably a hundred or more," answered Jamie airily. "I was too busy to count them."

"Is it dangerous?"

Jamie tossed his head. "It's shocking dangerous," he answered. "Once I was sculping a pup and the old swile come out of her hole and nearly sculped *me*. It was a shouting tangle, me boy. But I whacked her a couple times with my gaff and had her hide too."

The children's eyes were bright as ice in the sunshine.

"What else exciting happened to you?" asked Dick. "Was you ever shipwrecked?"

Jamie raked his memory for more vicarious thrills. "No, but we got pinched up in the ice and had to blow ourselves out with blasting powder. Then there was the time we climbed atop an iceberg big as yon hill, and it began to roll and the water was churning around it."

"Then what?"

"Then what! It rolled clear over, of course, and I slid down into the water."

"Did you drown?" asked little Luddie fearfully.

"I would have," admitted Jamie, "but the captain's big dog

82

pulled me out. The captain, he's got a dog big as Daisy, and he gave him to me. It's really more like he gave me to the dog."

"When are you going to bring him here?" asked Meg.

The time Jamie dreaded had arrived. It wouldn't matter with the others, but how would Meg take it?

"I'm not staying here more than a few days," he explained. "The captain's going to take me home with him and I'm going to learn to be a fisherman."

Meg looked as if he had slapped her face. Her lips quivered and she lowered her head and began lacing her fingers.

"I want to be a sealer," cried Dick. "I want to run off to sea like you did."

Jamie raised his chest, clasped his hands behind his back, and stood on his tiptoes the better to glare down at the younger boy.

"Be cripes!" he exclaimed. "Swiling's a man's work, me boy, and not for little sprats like you."

"Oh, I don't mean now," said Dick humbly. "I mean when I'm big like you."

Meg raised her head. "Won't you come back here ever, Jamie?" she asked. "I know you're not one of us, but it always seemed to me like you was."

Before he could answer, Captain Wight and the Critch parents broke up their earnest conference. They shook hands as if they had just completed an important deal. The captain even slipped some bills from his snap purse into Mr. Critch's hand. "Buy something for the young ones," he suggested.

He turned to Jamie, "I'll be back for you in about three days," he said, "so don't change your mind."

83

"No indeed, sir. I'd never do that."

Jamie watched him climb into the cab. He hoped the captain wouldn't change his either, but right now it was pleasant to be back with the Critches.

"You young ones go help brake the wheels doing down," ordered Mr. Critch, "Not you, Jamie. I want a few words with you."

"I hope you don't think I'm ungrateful, sir," said Jamie. "Running off the way I did and now going off again."

Mr. Critch shook his head. "Us ones got to take our chance if we want to get ahead," he said. "And mostly we have to make our own chances. Like calling out the fish and hoping somebody will come out and buy. There's no honorable lordships waiting to hand us anything on a silver plate like some gets. But I'll miss you, lad. You were a good boy most of the time."

"How can you miss me when you've got so many others?" asked the boy with surprise.

Mr. Critch looked about helplessly as he sought for a way to explain. Then he stretched his hands out in front of Jamie.

"I've got ten fingers, you see," he said, "and maybe that's more than enough, but was I to lose even one under the cleaver, I'd miss it awful."

Jamie thought of Foggy. "A man aboard our ship had no toes because they were froze on the ice," he said, "but he gets along all right without them."

"But don't he miss them?"

"Yes, I believe he does," admitted Jamie. "He stuffs the toes of his shoes with paper sometimes, but it don't seem to help

84

much. I'll miss you, Mr. Critch, and Mrs. Critch and everybody."

"People like us ones got to part from our children when they get their chance," went on Mr. Critch. "Mother and I been talking about how Meg maybe ought to go into service in some rich home and learn to make her living. If we can't get work for the older ones, we'll have to go on poor relief soon."

Jamie seemed to fit right back into the Critch family. He would have felt that he had never left if it wasn't for the questions of his adventures asked by the family. And the tales he told would have done credit to the imaginations of the men 'tweendecks.

"But don't it seem a cruel thing to kill the seals?" asked Meg as they were unloading some leftover fish from the wagon one evening. Before Jamie could answer, she said, "Put that big one aside. Mom wants it for fish and brewis."

Jamie gave Meg a superior look as he pulled the big fish from the pile. "We're hard people who live in a hard land," he explained. "We have to kill the seals if we want to eat."

"But we don't eat seals," said Meg. "We eat fish."

"Seals eat fish too," Jamie reminded her. "It's what the captain said, and you have to do sums to understand it."

It was late morning on the day that Captain Wight returned for Jamie, and Sailor was with him. The big dog sat on the seat of the carriage as if he were used to its elegance.

"It's out we go, Sailor," said the captain at the bottom of the hill, "and you might as well wait here, cabbie, to save us the push and pull."

Captain Wight climbed the hill with Sailor following him.

Near the top, he was surrounded by Critches again. This time all of their attention was for the dog.

"It's Sailor," cried little Luddie. "That's what Jamie said his name was."

Dick sniffed. "He's not so big," he said scornfully. "Jamie said he was big as a horse."

But the younger children thought him so enormous that they burst into howls of fright and ran for the safety of the stairs.

Mr. Critch had just returned from the wharf with his day's supply of fresh fish.

"The boy's here," he told Captain Wight, "and my wife's put his clothes through three washings so he'll be clean for the trip. Dick, you run and fetch Jamie and his nightshirt."

When Sailor caught sight of Jamie, the frightened little Critches thought that he was going to eat the boy. The dog barked wildly and jumped at him. He knocked Jamie to his knees, then licked his face with joy.

It was some time before the boy could calm him down, but when Sailor realized that Jamie was going with him and the captain, he regained his old quiet dignity.

The older children and Mrs. Critch clustered around James Piercey for a last farewell. Mr. Critch turned a hopeful face to Captain Wight.

"Perhaps you'd like to take our Meg here along with you too," he suggested. "Her and Jamie work well together."

"No, no," declined the captain with alarm. "Jamie is enough, thank you."

Jamie immediately seized upon Mr. Critch's proposal. "Oh,

please, Captain, sir," he entreated. "Please can't we take Meg too?"

"One more never made a difference," pointed out Mr. Critch.

"It's not one more," countered the captain. "It's *three* more. My wife isn't even expecting the dog back."

Mrs. Critch joined in the argument and her agitation was quite apparent.

"No, not Meg," she cried, seizing the girl by the shoulders.

Captain Wight saw an ally in Mrs. Critch.

"Taking two of them would be kidnaping, ma'am," he agreed. "It would hurt my conscience."

"You know Meg's growing up to where she'll have to go off to work somewheres," pointed out Mr. Critch. "And Dick and Edna are big enough to help us now."

"But it's so sudden," protested Mrs. Critch. "We ought to take time to think it over."

Even as she spoke, the noonday gun boomed from Signal Hill. Captain Wight quickly pulled out his big gold watch and twisted the minute hand a fraction. "I must leave right away," he said, "so you'd better think it over for another year."

Then Meg stepped in front of him and began twisting her fingers in her skirt. Her eyes were filled with entreaty. "I'd be no trouble, sir," she said, "and I'd be a help to Mrs. Wight. I'd rather work for you than strangers down in town."

"Please take her now, Captain," begged Jamie again. "You could bring her back to see Mrs. Critch when you come to the sealing next March."

Captain Wight heaved a great sigh like steam escaping from a valve. He knew that he and Mrs. Critch had lost.

"As long as I'm taking one, I might as well make it a pair," he said in surrender.

"Can I go too?" cried Dick.

"Me too," Edna joined him.

Captain Wight raised his hand decisively. "No more Critches," he pronounced. "She's all I'll take."

To make sure that no more foster children would be wished on him, he hastened the leave-taking. "Fetch your belongings, Meg," he said. "Jamie's already got his nightshirt and the cabbie's waiting."

"I don't have much to fetch," said the girl as she ran lightly up the stairs, followed by her mother. When they returned, Meg was wearing a gray woolen shawl and carrying a bundle wrapped in newspaper and a geranium in a tin can.

"It belongs to me all by myself," she boasted, showing the plant to Captain Wight. "I got it out of a broken pot somebody threw in the alley."

Mrs. Critch sniffled. "Meg always did like pretty things," she explained, "and the geranium sort of cheered up the kitchen."

"Come, come," said the captain to hustle them. "The schooner will be waiting for us too."

He shook hands with Mr. and Mrs. Critch and waved to the children. Then he started down the hill alone so he would not have the pain of witnessing the family farewells. He hoped that Mrs. Critch might find it too much of a wrench to part with Meg and the geranium. But the mother was stoical, although tears rolled down her hollow cheeks.

Meg soon reached the captain's side, the geranium clutched

88

to her breast. She changed it to the crook of the arm carrying the bundle and trustfully took the captain by the hand.

"You're a brave man, aren't you?" she asked, thinking of the perils of life at sea as recounted by Jamie.

"That I be," admitted the captain heartily, thinking of how he would have to face Sarah when he reached home.

Jamie gave one last look at the home that had been his for years. His last sight was of Mr. Critch bringing the side of his right hand down sharply against two fingers of his left.

VIII

Homeward Ho!

The surrounding hills shut off the wind from St. John's harbor, so six men rowing a longboat towed the small schooner toward the Narrows.

She was even older than the *Polar Star* and more wave-worn. Her beams creaked and her decks sagged. She had never known the power of steam. She was used to carrying such cargo as the barrels of flour, puncheons of molasses, Tom Boggan's new trap net, and even the boxes of store-bought shoes which filled part of her hatches now. Every man returning to his isolated outport was taking back another year's supply of staples which he had purchased in St. John's.

Meg had carefully set her geranium upon a hatchway cover. She stood at the railing with Jamie, watching the sights of the busy harbor. Sailor was between them. When the boy leaned to point at the English warship with its bristling guns, the dog growled under his breath and yanked at his jacket. But when

Meg hung over to wave to the crew of another schooner, he only fastened his eyes upon her warily.

When they reached the mouth of the Narrows, Meg stretched herself farther across the railing and began waving frantically.

"Good-bye, Mom!" she shouted. "Good-bye, Pa and Dick and Edna and—" She burst into tears before she could finish the litany of Critch names.

"What's wrong with you?" asked Jamie. "You sorry you came?"

After a few brief convulsive sobs, Meg wiped her eyes with a corner of her shawl. "No," she said. "I was just telling them good-bye."

But Jamie noticed that she lost interest in the voyage as soon as they were out on the open sea.

"Look, Meg," he began, hoping to entertain her. He pointed up at the masts. "They're putting on more sail. Many's the time I've helped set sail too."

Meg stared at the great white wings of canvas through tear-blurred eyes. "Looks like the wash hanging out on Monday," she said. "Edna'll be hanging out the wash now instead of me."

"Your ma's sheets aren't anywheres as big as those sails," said Jamie, irritated that Meg kept brooding over the past instead of facing this glorious new future with his own enthusiasm.

One of the crew up on the mast shouted, "Iceberg off starboard." There was a carefree note in his voice, because he was giving interesting information to those below instead of crying a warning.

"Looky!" Jamie exclaimed. "There it is, over there."

They raced to the other side of the ship, Sailor following on their heels.

The iceberg was far off. With its jagged peaks and smooth sides it looked like a white castle.

"That's like the big berg I climbed," boasted Jamie. "Gosh, when I was up at the top I could almost see the whole world. I could see the *Polar Star* anyway, and she was miles and miles away. If I was up on that berg now, I could look down and see this ship, and it wouldn't look no bigger than that box over there."

They watched the white iceberg rising out of the gray sea, and for a while Meg was silenced by wonderment. Then she said, "Remember, Pa used to tell us sometimes there was a berg off St. John's, but we never got to see it because the houses shut off the harbor. You think pa can see this iceberg, Jamie?"

"Of course not. We've left St. John's way behind."

The sea grew rougher as they moved up the lonely, rugged shoreline, which looked as remote as the iceberg. The ship began to roll and pitch more violently. Cold salty spray showered the children, so they moved away from the rail.

"It's rocking so, my geranium might get spilled," said Meg. She went to the hatchway and picked up the flower can. Then she pulled her shawl closer, sat down, and cuddled the geranium in her lap. She sat there watching the sea rise into a mountain on one side, then sink below the gunwales only to rise on the other side. She was thinking of what Jamie had said about St. John's being so far away. Every swell was pushing it farther behind them.

"I don't feel so good," she said after a while. "I want to go downstairs."

"It's not downstairs," Jamie corrected her. "It's 'below.'"

"Then I want to go underneath," insisted Meg.

Jamie led her to the open hatchway and down the ladder.

"This staircase sure is steep," complained Meg as she clung to the siderope with one hand and the geranium with the other. "It's worse than ours at home."

"It isn't a staircase," Jamie informed her. "It's called a ladder."

In the main cabin they met Tom Boggan poring over some old newspapers.

"Meg feels bad," Jamie informed him.

"I want to lie down somewheres by myself," Meg added.

"No, no, little girl," said Tom. "That's the worst thing you could do. You ought to go back on deck and stay in the fresh air."

Meg stubbornly shook her head. "I want to lie down and be alone," she repeated. "I don't want to watch that water going up and down no more."

Tom obligingly led her into a tiny cabin and pointed out a bunk covered with a blanket. "This is where you'll sleep tonight," he said.

He and Jamie stood watching her for a few moments as she settled down. But she turned her back toward them and buried her face in the blanket. In a muffled voice she repeated, "I want to be alone."

"She doesn't seem too bad off," said Tom, "so we might as well go up on deck. How'd you like to steer this schooner, Jamie?"

"Steer her?" asked the boy, remembering the brawny men at the twin wheels of the *Polar Star*. "You mean me at the wheel all by myself?"

"The helmsman and I will be standing by," said Tom as they left the cabin.

"Will the captain of this schooner let me?" asked Jamie incredulously.

"We won't tell him until you learn how," said Tom. "He's going over some inventories with Captain Wight."

The two of them stepped out on deck; then Tom led the way aft. Jamie tried to keep from trembling because Tom might think it was fright.

An old seaman with a wooden leg was standing at the wheel. When Tom told him that Jamie wanted a turn, he only grunted and grinned. He stepped aside. Then because of the awe which paralyzed the boy for a moment, Tom seized Jamie's hands and set them on the wheel.

He pointed to the compass. "Keep her headed north-northeast," he ordered. "Watch the lubber's line."

Jamie was glad that he had worked so hard learning about the compass from Captain Wight. But he found it harder to keep a straight course than he had thought. It had looked so easy in the pilothouse of the *Polar Star*.

The lubber's line began moving away from the north-northeast point. Like most beginners, Jamie focused on the compass and tried to bring its point toward the lubbers line. But the needle was immovable. The ship yawed from side to side as Jamie frantically turned the wheel first one way then the other.

"Watch the lubber's line!" shouted the wooden-legged helmsman. "You want to go all over the ocean?" He started to grab the wheel, but Tom stopped him.

"Let the boy learn by himself," he said.

Sweat broke out on Jamie's face. He took his tongue between his teeth and steadied his hands. He felt as if he had to force his will on the wheel, down the chains, and back to the heavy rudder itself. He was its mind and he would make it obey.

"What's the matter with that confounded helmsman?" came the roar of the schooner captain's voice across the deck. "Has he gone to sleep. I never—" The voice stopped right above Jamie's head.

Captain Wight was with him. His face broke into a wide grin. "Well, be cripes, if it isn't the little landlubber chasing the compass card," he exclaimed with a chortle. He turned to the other captain. "This is my boy," he boasted.

Jamie knew that he had to make good now. Two captains were watching him.

The boy's fingers relaxed. He kept his eyes on the lubber's line and his hands firm on the wheel. He almost felt as if his own arms were back under the water steadying the rudder. Slowly he turned the wheel until the lubber's line settled at north-northeast. He had the feel of it.

"Now there's a bright boy for you," said Captain Wight as if it had all been his idea. "That's what comes from teaching them young. Too bad we can't lawfully take them on the sealers anymore."

Jamie's head was swimming in pride.

"I can steer, sir," he said to Captain Wight. "I could have steered the *Polar Star* for you."

As he looked backward, the lubber's line veered sharply to the left and the schooner lunged. Jamie's face reddened as he turned his attention to the wheel and steadied the course again.

The schooner captain put one hand beside Jamie's on the wheel. "That's enough for the first time, boy," he said. "We'll let you take another turn later."

Jamie reluctantly turned the wheel over to the one-legged helmsman. He joined Captain Wight and the two of them walked toward the railing.

"Captain, sir," said Jamie. "I really want to be a sailor. I still don't want to kill seals, but I want to go to sea with you and run the ship."

The captain brought his hand down on Jamie's shoulder with fierce pride. "Spoken like a skipper's boy," he declared. "But you'll still get your schooling first. Then you'll go to sea with me and I'll teach you everything you'll need to know." He changed the subject. "How's the little girl coming along? I heard she was sick, but when I went into the cabin she seemed all right. Maybe she's just lonely. You'd better go down and cheer her up. I'm not much of a hand with girls. Never been around them much."

Jamie rushed down to cheer Meg with the news that he had actually been steering the ship. Did she notice that its course was wobbly at first but then got smooth and sure?

He burst into the cabin. "Meg, Meg," he cried. "I was steering this ship—all by myself."

Meg rose to a sitting position. "I thought it was going funny for a while," she said.

"But then it kept a straight course," said Jamie. "Soon as

97

I got the feel of it, I kept it right on point."

"That was sure smart of you."

"And now the captain's going to teach me to be a real sailor
. . . when I'm done with school."

He waited for words of praise from Meg, but she only said,
"I wonder what they're doing at home now."

Jamie was annoyed at her.

"You aren't seasick," he declared. "You're just homesick. And
I can tell you what they're doing. They're wondering what we're
doing, and talking about how we're having a big time sailing
on a schooner out on the water. And if they thought we were
blubbering and acting homesick, they'd be wonderful sad,
wouldn't they? Come up on deck, Meg."

"I guess you're right," the girl admitted. "I wouldn't want
Mom and Pa to feel bad about me."

They returned to the deck, where Jamie led Meg back to
show her the wheel which he had handled all by himself.

"Little girl feeling better?" asked Captain Wight.

"She wasn't really sick," said Jamie. "She was just homesick."

Meg lowered her head and twisted the ends of her shawl in
embarrassment.

"Now, now," said the captain. "We don't want that kind of
sickness on this ship." He searched his mind for a suitable
remedy. "I'm thinking of a treat for you," he continued. "See
that little keg stowed near the sled? It's some preserved tamarinds from the West Indies. A company official gave them to
me as a gift because I brought in such a big cargo of sculps.
I was taking it home to Sarah, but I'll have it opened right now
so you young ones can have a treat."

A member of the crew pulled the keg out and began prying it open. Meanwhile Jamie took Meg aft and showed her the wheel.

"You mean you drive this whole big boat with that?" asked the girl.

"You don't drive it. You steer it. And I can tell you it's not easy as it looks. Nothing like driving Daisy."

Jamie wanted to show Meg right then and there, but Captain Wight was beckoning to them. "It's open," he called. "Come and get your fill."

The tamarinds, small and withered as prunes, were clustered on their stems and covered with a thick dark syrup. Captain Wight gingerly fished one out and held it over the keg.

"Here, Meg," he said. "Take this one. You have to eat them off the stem. And bend over the keg. They're messy."

Jamie picked out his own cluster and let the syrup drip from it. Then he fastened his teeth into one of the brown tamarinds. It had a strange, sweet taste which was most pleasant. The syrup made it taste even better.

The children helped themselves until their hands and chins were sticky. They spat the seeds across the railing in a competition for distance. From time to time they would offer Sailor a tamarind, but he wrinkled his nose with distaste.

Suddenly Meg dropped a half-finished cluster back into the keg. A greenish pallor spread over her face.

"I—I'm sick," she groaned. "I'm really sea—sick—I—think."

She dashed to the rail and hung over it.

Jamie quickly finished his cluster and carefully put the top on the keg to end all temptation. He certainly didn't want the humiliation of getting seasick himself after he had made such a reputation at the wheel.

Sailor sank to his paws and whined unhappily. Something was wrong with Meg that couldn't be righted by a brave Newfoundland dog.

Captain Wight was annoyed with himself for giving the preserved fruit to the children on the ocean trip when Meg had already been suspected of seasickness.

"Sarah would have known better," he admitted to Tom Boggan. "Women know how to handle girl children."

"Children are queer ones," admitted Tom. "I haven't got the knack of handling my brother's children yet. That Jack is a handful and he isn't a girl."

Late that night the schooner dropped anchor in the bay of Sample's Harbour and waited in the thin fog for morning. Meg had recovered, although she was still a little pale from her bout with the tamarinds.

The children could not leave until all the cargo had been rowed ashore in the longboat. They impatiently watched barrels and boxes being lowered by the winches. When the keg of tamarinds went down, Meg made a face.

"If my brother got the message," Tom told the captain, "he'll be waiting on the dock for us with the horse and wagon."

"If not," decided Captain Wight, "we'll walk to Spanish Choice and bring the cargo over tomorrow."

It wasn't necessary to make this arrangement. Tom's brother, an older man with a slight stoop to his shoulders, was in the little group of curious Sample's Harbour residents.

100

"Thought you'd never get here," he said peevishly. "Thought you'd sunk."

"We got held up in St. John's," said Tom as he grabbed for the line cast from the dock.

"Had to collect two new crew members," called the captain as the boat was moored. He looked sharply at Sailor, then at the other men on the dock. "And how is the honorable William Cotter?" he queried. "Busy as ever?"

"Not right now," answered a gnarled old man with only one tooth in his mouth. "He's gone on vacation."

"I'm glad to hear that," rejoiced the captain. "He deserves it—the hardworking, conscientious man. How long will he be gone?"

"A month I heard," put in another. "He's visiting his son in the States."

"A good climate for the bilious," pronounced the captain. "He should stay longer."

Tom's brother drove the horse and wagon onto the dock, and the men standing around obligingly helped to haul the barrels, boxes, and the trap net to the wagon.

The captain and Tom's brother sat on the seat with Meg between them. She had set the geranium under the seat. Tom and Jamie rode barrels in the back, and Sailor followed behind the wagon.

When they drove away from the dock and started up the ridge road, the fog was lifting. The narrow road curved along the shore, almost level with the water in places. Towering above them on the shore side were high flat ridges of rock and barrens.

101

The ground on both sides of the roadway was covered with a wild growth. Juniper, wild berry bushes, mosses, and muskeg pressed flat against the earth. Here and there a sole tamarack or pine fought for survival against the wind. But in the hidden valleys, which they came upon unexpectedly, there were heavy forests of black spruce.

Meg was enjoying the ride and the country sights. But still she could not forget the life she had left behind.

"This is just like the fish wagon, isn't it?" she called back to Jamie. On sudden impulse she jumped to her feet, cupped her hands to her lips, and chanted in a nasal singsong, "Fi-i-ish! Fresh fi-i-ish! Come youse, come youse, fish for brewis!"

She sat down again and primly straightened her skirt across her knees.

IX

Mrs. Wight

The creak of the wagon and the crunch of the horse's hoofs brought Mrs. Wight to the door. She was wearing a new brown cotton dress and a daisy-white apron in anticipation of her husband's return. But as a sailor's wife she did not greet her husband with an outburst of emotion upon his return from a long cruise.

"It's good to have you back, Heber," was her matter-of-fact greeting, but her eyes glowed with happiness.

The captain had no such reserve. He jumped from the wagon, lifted her by the waist, and swung her around. "It's good to be back, me beautiful girl," he cried. Then he planted a whiskery kiss on her lips.

"Now, Heber, indeed to goodness," said Mrs. Wight in a flustered voice. "Such carrying on in front of everybody. Did you have a good trip?"

"The best yet," said the captain. "The company commended

me highly. And I've brought back the pair of laced shoes you wanted. If they're a little too large, you can stuff some paper in them like my steward does."

Mrs. Wight gave a quick smile to the Boggan men and the children. She supposed that the boy and girl were with the Boggans. But at sight of Sailor coming from behind the wagon, she looked worried.

"You couldn't find anybody to take him?" she asked.

"I've found him a master all right," replied her husband. "It's the boy here. Come down, Jamie, and shake hands with Mrs. Wight."

The captain's wife took Jamie's hand in hers. "My, you're a fine boy," she said. "Where do you and your sister live?"

Meg, geranium in hand, saved the captain an explanation.

"We're going to live here, ma'am," she said. "That's why we come."

"And this is Meg," said the captain quickly. "She'll be a big help to you."

Still Mrs. Wight could not understand the situation. "You're moving into Spanish Choice," she decided. "You're friends of the Boggans."

Captain Wight cleared his throat vigorously. "They're friends, all right, Sarah," he said, "but they're going to live with us."

Meg wasn't sure whether she liked this plump little woman or not. She didn't have the tired, careworn look of a mother.

"May I get some water somewheres for my geranium, ma'am?" she asked. "It looks a little wilty."

Mrs. Wight's attention was drawn to the flower. Her face brightened.

104

"What a beautiful flower!" she said. "We'll have to keep it on the parlor table while you're visiting."

"They aren't visiting, Sarah, me darling," said the captain. "They've come to stay. I brought them home for us to raise."

Mrs. Wight appeared to be quite baffled for a few moments. "Well, indeed to goodness!" was all she could say. Then she impulsively gathered Meg within the curve of one arm and Jamie into the other, although the boy stiffened and blushed. Mrs. Critch had never hugged him.

"Better to get children late than never," said Mrs. Wight. "Welcome to your new home." Then over their heads she gave her husband a perplexed look. "Where did you get them?" she asked him. "Out of an orphan asylum?"

"No," answered the captain, "but there's plenty more where they came from."

Meg broke from the woman's embrace. "You're squeezing the geranium, ma'am," she cautioned. "And if you'll please tell me where the water be, I'll take it there."

"There's some in a bucket by the back door, dearie," said Mrs. Wight. "Just go around." She quickly regained her poise. "Now, I know you're all hungry," she said in a practical manner, "and it's good I cooked plenty of pork and potatoes. Put the things in the shed, Heber, then come on in. I'll have everything on the table in no time."

It was after dinner when Mrs. Wight was filling a bowl with leftovers for Sailor that she brought up the main problem. "But the dog," she said to her husband, who had joined her in the kitchen. "You can't keep him here."

Captain Wight mischievously untied the bow at her back,

and the apron fell to the floor. Meg, scraping the dishes, giggled as she picked it up and tied it around the woman's waist again.

"Now don't you go worrying your pretty head over my problems, me girl," said the captain to his wife. "I'll solve this one. I've got a month to do it in."

He secretly hoped that he would be successful. There seemed only one solution and Sarah wasn't likely to agree to it.

While Jamie carried the bowl out to Sailor, Mrs. Wight began washing the dishes. Meg promptly took a dish towel from the rack.

"This sure is a pretty house," she said to Mrs. Wight, "and everything so handy. Where do I sleep tonight? With you or on the floor?"

"Let's see." Mrs. Wight pondered with a serving platter half submerged in the soapy water. "We could set up a cot in the parlor. No, not the parlor. The little back room where I do my sewing will be just right, and there's already a couch in it. And Jamie can put up in the loft where the captain keeps his tools and things. I'll lay a feather bed on the floor for him. That will be all right for a boy."

Captain Wight made a cautious observation. "Looks like the house is too small for us now, Sarah," he said.

"That it does," admitted his wife. "Maybe you could build on a new room, now that you're home for a while."

Captain Wight scratched his beard. "Perhaps we ought to move somewhere else," he suggested. "Build a big new house across the bay on that piece of land I once thought of buying."

Mrs. Wight was so shocked that she dropped the platter into

the water. "Leave our house here?" she gasped. "Our house we've lived in ever since we got married?"

The captain stared at the wall, then ran his hand over it.

"Look how the wallpaper's worn," he said. "And the paint is faded outside. It's the first thing I noticed when I got home. We really ought to move into a new house."

Mrs. Wight's eyes snapped. "What nonsense, Heber! All you need do is repaper and put on a new coat of paint. You'll have time for that too."

"It was just a suggestion," said the captain humbly, "and there's the problem of the dog. He'd be legal in that cove across the bay. And you'd be closer to a town."

"I'm close enough to Spanish Choice," replied his wife, "and you never should have brought the dog back. Why didn't you give him to someone on the ship as you said? You know Sailor would be as content with one person as another, long as he was well treated."

"No, Sarah, it's different now. Sailor's devoted to Jamie. Even saved his life off Labrador. I'll tell you about it later."

Mrs. Wight whirled around and pointed a dripping fork at the captain's nose. "Heber Wight," she announced, "I can tell you that I'm not moving out of this house."

Meg, who had been silent all through the argument, finally spoke. "We had to move out of a house once because Pa couldn't pay the rent," she offered, "and Mom sure cried. Now she'd cry if she had to move from that place in the alley."

Then the girl began sobbing into the dish towel herself. Mrs. Wight quickly put her arms around Meg.

107

"What's wrong, dearie?" she asked. "Don't you feel well?"

Captain Wight knew what was wrong. "She's homesick," he said. "She's been that way off and on."

Mrs. Wight gave her a squeeze. "She's just tired out and lonesome because everything is new," she said. "Come with me, Meg, and help me tidy up the sewing room for you. Then you can go down and watch the fishing boats, or maybe you and Jamie can play with the children at Tom Boggan's. Then tomorrow you can help around the house."

"They'll be going to school tomorrow," corrected Captain Wight. "They've missed too much already, and Tom's young nephews are coming by for them."

"As you say, Heber," said Mrs. Wight obediently. She was willing to be a dutiful wife and give in to her husband's wishes so long as they did not concern moving from her house.

That night as she and Meg made up the couch in the sewing room she noticed that the girl was unusually silent. She sat down on the couch and drew Meg toward her.

"You'll get to like it here, Meg," she said. "I know you're homesick now and I know just how you feel. It's the way I felt when I first got married and left my family. Used to cry myself to sleep sometimes when I thought about them. But when you grow up, you've got to make changes and get to like them. You can't always stay a child at home."

Meg leaned her red curls against Mrs. Wight's large, soft shoulder. She decided that she liked her after all. She liked her very much. If Mrs. Wight had really been her mother, she could have loved her.

Tom's nephew, Jack Boggan, appeared at the Wight door early because it was a long walk around the cove to the school. With him was little Billy, who was finishing his first year.

The children eyed each other appraisingly. Jamie thought that Jack with his smiling, freckled face and the cleft in his upper teeth looked like a "gert" fellow, as John Noseworthy would have said. But he felt that anybody related to Tom would have to be a great fellow.

Jack approved of Jamie, although he was suspicious of his city background. He had no feelings whatever about Meg. She was just a girl and didn't matter. But Billy smiled up at Meg when she took his hand.

"I've got a little brother just like you," she told him, "but I had to leave him because I'm growing up."

As they started away Sailor joined them.

"Stay home!" Jamie ordered. "You can't come to school. It's not for dogs."

Little Billy fearfully pressed against Meg's shawl.

"He won't hurt you," said Meg. "He'll like you if you like him. That's the way dogs are."

Captain and Mrs. Wight were standing on the porch, watching the leave-taking.

"Take him along, Jamie," suggested Mrs. Wight. "He can wait outside for you."

"He'll carry your books home," added the captain. "Wait until I get a strap to wrap around them. And he can carry your lunches there."

Mrs. Wight had packed jam sandwiches, raisins, and a bottle

109

of tea into two tin biscuit boxes. The captain strapped the boxes together, and Sailor dutifully carried the end of the strap in his mouth.

"The captain's dog sure is smart," said Jack.

"He isn't the captain's dog anymore," said Jamie loftily. "He belongs to me now."

Sailor bore witness to this by following Jamie closely.

The city children were still amazed at the great open spaces of the outport country.

"The ocean is bigger here than at St. John's," said Jamie.

"And the ground's emptier," said Meg. "But look at all those trees down in the valley. I never saw so many trees together even in the park at home."

The road went between stone walls and fences made of longers—long peeled spruce poles. It crossed many rock-bridged culverts. On the water side little brown "beachie" birds glided over the bracken.

Jamie and Meg stopped to look at the rocky cliffs on their right.

"I never saw so much rock," remarked Jamie.

Jack explained. "Uncle Tom says that when God finished making the world He had a lot of rocks left over, so He dumped them on Newfoundland. And Uncle Tom thinks this is where He dumped most of them. But if we don't hurry, we'll be late, and Miss Polly will take the stick to us."

"Will she be our teacher?" asked Jamie.

"She's everybody's teacher," said Jack, "even Billy's."

"I can spell," put in Billy, getting over his bashfulness. "H-e-n, coopie. P-i-g, chookie, and d-o-g, Sailor."

110

Jack burst out laughing. "Miss Polly didn't teach him that," he explained. "It was Uncle Tom."

"What's a coopie?" asked Meg.

"It's a hen," said Jack scornfully. "Haven't you ever seen a hen?" He was beginning to have a low opinion of city children.

"What's a chookie?" asked Jamie.

"Haven't you ever seen a pig?"

"I never heard them called that," admitted Jamie.

"Then I suppose you never heard Sailor called a dog."

Jamie's face flushed with irritation. "And I suppose you've never heard about bedlamers and doters and rusties," he retorted.

"What are they?" asked Jack in turn.

"Seals, of course. S-e-a-l, swile. I learned all about them when I went sealing with the captain. I bet you've never gone swiling."

"And I bet you've never gone fishing," returned Jack. "And I bet you can't row or scull a boat."

Jamie stuck his nose in the air. "Be cripes, me boy," he said, imitating the captain. "Who wants to do that when he can steer a big schooner? I can steer by the compass and I know all the compass points—north, north by east—"

Meg interrupted him. "I bet none of you can bathe a baby or cook a brewis or iron a shirt right. Everybody knows how to do different things, so nobody's smarter than anybody else."

Jamie and Jack felt admonished.

They were approaching the school now. It was a large square dwelling that had been converted into a schoolhouse. When the children went inside, they could see where the partitions had been removed to make one large room. The pupils sat in groups of five at long tablelike desks, and the teacher's desk was on a raised platform.

Jamie did not have to feel ashamed that he was only in the third reader because there were boys even older who were no further advanced. Children in the outports attended school as irregularly as he had. Many of the older boys had already left with the fishing schooners for the Grand Banks or had dropped schooling for good.

The first day went quickly for both Jamie and Meg. They did sums in the morning, and both of them were good at arithmetic. After the lunch recess, during which some of the children even took rides on Sailor, they filed back to their chairs. Miss Polly Thistle presided over their reading and gave them exercises in penmanship.

The latter was the most difficult and uninteresting subject as far as Jamie was concerned.

"Don't move your wrist," Miss Polly admonished him. "Use your whole arm."

And what was the use of it? A sailor didn't have to write. Or did he? The boy suddenly remembered entries in the ship's log made by Captain Wight in a handwriting as dainty and graceful as the threads of a spider web.

The day seemed to go faster than those school days in St. John's.

"I told you Sailor would still be waiting for us," said Jamie when it let out, "and there he is."

Sailor was given the strap bulging with books and tablets to carry home.

112

"I saw a red wagon in the shed that would be just right for him," said Jamie. "Maybe we can hitch it to him tomorrow."

A second look revealed that there was not only a wagon but the harness which Captain Wight had made. It was cut from canvas, and the collar was padded with dried grass.

X

Rocks

Jamie felt as if he slept in a room of wonders. The loft was almost like a ship's cabin with the old spyglasses, sextants, and dog-eared charts lying around. But there were also carpentry tools and a work table where the captain often sawed and hammered.

The boy liked to stand by the front window of the loft and look through a spyglass.

"It was real foggy yesterday, but I can see the lighthouse way down the point today," he told Captain Wight early one morning. "I can even see a lady coming out. She's shaking a tablecloth and all the seagulls are flying around her."

"Then it's six-thirty," said the captain, checking his watch. "She always comes out to shake the tablecloth at exactly six-thirty."

He returned the watch to his pocket and resumed sharpening a kitchen knife with his whetstone.

114

"I can see Cuddy's Cove across the bay, too, and all the fish stages and sheds," continued Jamie. "Some men are getting into a trapboat. Tom Boggan's going to take me out to his next Saturday. The Boggan men go out to Tom's net a couple times a day and bring back the fish caught in it."

He swung the glass to the right. "And there's a pretty, flat place farther on with a sandy beach and a waterfall coming down the cliff. I'd like to row over there someday."

"The best piece of land on the bay," said the captain. "Private but close to Cuddy's. I was going to buy that land and build my house there. That was the biggest mistake of my life. If this house was setting over there, Sailor would be safe and you children closer to the Sample's Harbour School."

Jamie imagined the captain's trim yellow and green house sitting back from the sandy beach. There was room for a garden, and the waterfall from the cliff could furnish all the water needed.

"Too bad you can't sail it over there same as a boat," he said. "Too bad you can't put a deck under it and sails on the roof, and steer it right across the bay. It isn't too far."

Captain Wight put down the knife and stone and joined Jamie at the window. He jerked the spyglass from his hand and pressed an eye to it himself. He moved it back and forth across the bay.

"High tide and the approach would be good," he said. "The smooth slope would help and it's clear of big rocks."

He began humming as he went back to the table. He plucked a hair from his beard and slit it with the knife's blade. "She's

115

sharp enough," he commented. "Sharp as your mind, me boy."

He went down the steep steps that were so like a ship's ladder. Jamie soon followed him because he knew that it was time to get ready for school. He joined Meg and both of them hitched Sailor to the little wagon.

When they returned to the front of the house, they saw Captain Wight examining the foundation of the house very closely.

"It takes a mess of rocks to hold up the house, doesn't it?" the boy commented.

"Lashins of them, as John Noseworthy would say," agreed the captain, "and I carried most of them myself. But it was good for me. Made muscle."

"I'd hate to make muscle that way," confessed Jamie. "I'd rather get strong rowing a boat."

Jack Boggan was in a mischievous mood when he joined them. On the way to school he tried to mix up little Billy when he recited the alphabet for them. He picked foxgrass and tickled Meg's ears with it. He kicked pebbles at Jamie.

Half a mile out from Spanish Choice the road rose steeply above the bay, which was screened by a stretch of shaggy spruce. As the children passed, they heard the creak of oarlocks in the hidden water below.

"There's a boat down there," said Jack. "I wonder who's in it?"

He picked up a stone and shied it over the top of the trees. They could hear the splash below. Copying his brother, Billy picked up a handful of pebbles and tossed them, but they only dusted the trees.

Jamie took a stone in each hand and aimed them across the

117

treetops. He heard a hollow splash and the dull thud of wood.

Meg giggled.

Then an angry voice rose from the hidden boat. "You fellows cut that out! I'm coming up and get you!"

Jack stiffened with fright and his face paled. "That's Uncle Tom," he gasped. "Run!"

The excitement was shared by Sailor. He barked sharply as he followed the children's flying feet, the lunches and books in the wagon bouncing behind him.

"Shut up!" Jack hissed at the dog. "You want to give us away?"

They silently hurried on to school with heads downcast. But once in the schoolroom, they became so busy studying that they forgot their mischief.

It wasn't until late that afternoon when they were almost home that they remembered it. Tom Boggan was standing in the road ahead of them. There was something ominous in the way he was holding two rocks.

The children slowed down. So did Sailor.

"Hello, Uncle Tom," said Jack innocently.

Tom Boggan did not return the greeting. He began juggling the rocks.

"You catch many fish in your new net?" asked Jamie. "I'm waiting to help you Saturday."

Tom Boggan spoke. "You little sprats think you're smart throwing rocks down at a defenseless man in a boat, don't you?"

"How do you know it was us?" asked Jack. "Maybe it was somebody else."

"Who else would be on the road with a dog that's the only one in the cove?"

118

"D-o-g spells Sailor," piped up Billy.

Tom weighed the rock in his right hand with great deliberation.

"I'll give you boys a head start," he told them. "I'll count to ten and you better run fast. Meg, you hold Sailor and stand behind me. You, too, Billy."

Jamie and Jack immediately took his advice. They raced down the road as if their lives depended on it. At the fateful count of "ten" Jack heard a rock thud behind his flying heels. Another well-placed one landed behind Jamie. They fled faster, just a few steps ahead of the small dust clouds raised by Tom's broadside of rocks. At last they were out of range.

"My goodness to me, you must have hurried home from school," Mrs. Wight called from the front of the house where she was planting flower seeds. "You're early. Where's Meg and Sailor?"

"They're coming," said Jamie. "They got held up."

"Want me to stay around awhile and help you plant the flowers?" asked Jack. "I don't feel like going home yet."

When a whole day went by without any mention from the Wights about the rock throwing, Jamie thought he was safe. But he was worried as to whether Tom would take him to the trap on Saturday.

Two evenings later, when he went past the shed to get water from the spring, he heard a low "p-s-st! p-s-st!" from the rock wall. He turned to see Captain Wight beckoning to him. The boy went to him.

The captain was acting in a furtive manner. "Sarah isn't anywhere outside, is she?" he asked in a whisper.

"No, sir," answered Jamie. "She's in the kitchen trying a new dress on Meg."

Captain Wight dropped his secretive manner and the whispering.

"So you've been throwing rocks at Tom Boggan," he bawled.

Jamie was startled. His active mind sought for an excuse.

"He threw rocks at us too," he said lamely.

"Jamie," said the captain sternly, "never try to dilute the truth. You threw the rocks first at him down in his boat. You might have hit him on the head and killed him. And he never would hurt you, because he can aim a rock as straight as he can shoot a gun."

Jamie's lips felt cold. He had never thought of anything like killing Tom. He hung his head. He was filled with shame and remorse. Tom Boggan had been his best friend on the *Polar Star*.

"I never thought about hurting him," he said truthfully. "We just did it for fun."

"Since that's your idea of fun," said the captain, "I've figured out just the right punishment for you."

"Yes, sir, Captain," replied Jamie. He would show that he could take punishment like a man anyway.

"Next Saturday," continued the captain, "you'll be free all day to heave rocks. We'll row across the bay early in the morning and begin building a rock foundation on that piece of land we were looking at through the glass. It will be plenty of fun because it will take plenty of rocks."

Jamie knew he wouldn't have to wonder anymore about going

120

with Tom to the fish trap. But perhaps it would be fun to row across the bay with Captain Wight.

"Are you really going to build a new house there?" he asked. "What will Mrs. Wight say?"

The captain frowned. "Not a word about this to her," he ordered. "You wouldn't want her to know you were throwing rocks at Tom, would you?"

"Oh, no, sir," agreed Jamie.

"And you aren't to mention it to Meg either," said the captain. "She and Sarah are getting pretty thick, and you know how women are when they get together."

"Indeed I do," said Jamie.

"We'll take Sailor and the wagon across for hauling the rocks," continued the captain.

"Won't Mrs. Wight and Meg wonder what we're doing?" asked the boy.

"In that case, Jamie, we have no choice but to dilute the truth and tell them we're cutting firewood down the valley."

Jamie's eyes sparkled. "And will you let me row the skiff across?" he asked. That much of it would be fun anyway.

"No, me boy," said the captain. "You've got to save your strength for lifting the rocks."

XI

The Voyage of
Captain Wight's House

For two weeks Captain Wight busied himself taking measurements of the house and studying it from various angles.

Mrs. Wight, watching his activities, said, "It shouldn't take more than one coat. And maybe I'd like a darker shade of green this time."

One day the captain went into the sewing room where his wife was putting the last touches on a new woolen coat for Meg.

"Come out, Sarah," he said. "I want to show you something."

Mrs. Wight moved away from Meg. "Get the buttons out of the drawer while I'm gone," she said to the girl. "I'll mark the place for them when I come back."

Meg went to the sewing box and Mrs. Wight followed the captain outside. He put his hand on her shoulders and turned her around. He pointed to the house.

"She'll go down the road all right," he said, "but the wheels won't be on it."

"I don't know what you're talking about," said Mrs. Wight. "Did you order the paint when you went to Sample's Harbour?"

"I better wait and see what the sea spray does to the walls."

"We don't get any spray this far from the water."

"As for the floors," the captain went on, "I looked at them again, and they're watertight as hatches. But I'll use empty barrels all the same to hold them high as possible."

Mrs. Wight was puzzled. "Whatever are you talking about? You won't need barrels for the painting. You've always used scaffolds before."

"I'm not talking about the paint job," said her husband. "I'm planning for the voyage across the bay."

Mrs. Wight was completely bewildered.

"Now, I don't understand at all," she declared. "What voyage across the bay?"

"The voyage of the house," said her husband. "What else would I be talking about? I'm going to sail her across the bay and anchor her to the rock foundation Jamie and I have finished near Cuddy's Cove."

Mrs. Wight angrily stepped away from him.

"Heber," she demanded, "what crazy notion is this?"

"There's nothing crazy about it," said her husband. "You don't want to give up the house. Sailor can't stay here because William Cotter is due back soon, and he'll hear about the dog that goes to school with the children. It wouldn't be right to let Sailor be separated from Jamie. And Jamie is now our boy who

123

has to live in the house with us. So the only solution is to move the house to a new location where there's no ordinance against dogs."

Mrs. Wight gasped for breath, enough breath to put an end to this.

"Heber Wight," she exploded, "have you lost your mind?"

"No, I have just found a piece of it I mislaid." His ire began to rise. "It's you who have no mind, Mrs. Wight. It is all very logical."

"Say what you want, Captain Wight," retorted his wife, "but I refuse to be a partner in such nonsense. Sail a house across the bay indeed!"

She turned on her heel and went marching back to the door. Even the bow on the back of her apron trembled with indignation.

Captain Wight stood with his arms akimbo and watched the bow disappear. It was the first big quarrel he'd had with Sarah since the time she had tried to make him give up the sailing trips.

He muttered under his breath savagely. He leaned over and picked up a rock. He hurled it against the house with all his might. He turned sharply, dug his fists into his coat pockets, and went stamping down the road to the fishing village.

Meg could see that something was wrong with Mrs. Wight when she returned to the sewing room. The woman's fingers trembled so that she couldn't thread a needle. Then she dropped the buttons on the floor.

"You feeling well, ma'am?" asked Meg.

"I'm all right," declared Mrs. Wight. "It's the captain. I just don't know what gets into men. You know what he wants to do?" Meg shook her head. "He wants to move this house. Sail it across the bay to Cuddy's Cove. I might have known he and Jamie weren't cutting wood with never a stick brought into this yard."

"What were they doing?" asked Meg with interest. She had felt a little slighted that she hadn't been invited on the outings.

"They've built a house foundation near Cuddy's Cove," explained Mrs. Wight. "And that explains why the captain went to Sample's Harbour on business. He's bought that land. Well, he can just plant it in cabbage and potatoes for all of me. Have you ever heard of such a ridiculous thing? Pulling a house loose and floating it across the water?"

"They moved a house on Clewe's Hill once," remembered Meg, "but they only put logs under it and rolled it down the street."

"I know they move houses, but they don't float them over the water."

"They put one of the fish sheds on a boat and rowed it down the cove," said Meg. "Jamie and I watched them do it."

"An old shed!" ejaculated Mrs. Wight. "What matter if it fell off and sank to the bottom? But suppose my house should sink?"

Meg looked down at a button she had picked from the floor.

"The captain sails those big ships down to Labrador through the ice and everything," she said. "Jamie told me how dangerous it is. But all those men on board trust him."

"I know it's dangerous going to the sealing grounds in the worst time of the year," said Mrs. Wight. "I tried to stop him long ago, but it was no use. Captain Wight is a stubborn man."

125

Meg studied the button in her hand. Then she raised her eyes and gave Mrs. Wight a level glance. "You be stubborn too, ma'am," she accused.

She immediately felt like biting her tongue. What would Mrs. Wight say to such impertinence? But the woman only said "ouch" and began sucking her finger.

"I pricked it," she explained. "I can't seem to do anything right today."

For the first time since his return Captain Wight was late to supper. After he had said the blessing, he lapsed into a gloomy silence.

Jamie tried to enliven the meal.

"I was throwing sticks for Sailor," he said, "and he jumped clear off a cliff to go after them."

"Enjoy Sailor while you have him," said Captain Wight glumly. "I heard at the wharf that William Cotter is back earlier than expected. He'll be coming over to get Sailor soon."

Jamie was horrified. "Get him!" he cried. "But he won't have the right now that we're moving over to Cuddy's Cove."

He slapped his hand over his mouth because he suddenly remembered that he wasn't to mention the work on the foundation to Mrs. Wight or Meg.

Captain Wight didn't seem to notice the slip.

"We aren't moving, Jamie," he said quietly. "We're staying here and you'll have to give up Sailor."

A great silence fell upon the table. Mrs. Wight abruptly rose to get more potatoes, although the bowl was nearly full. She stood by the stove for a long time.

126

Jamie was filled with desperation. He had the sudden urge to run away from the Wights as he had from the Critches and take Sailor with him. They could go back to St. John's but not to the Critches. With all the experience he now had, he could surely get a berth on a ship, one that would accept the dog. Then he thought how ungrateful that would be to the captain. If the *Polar Star* had been driven on the rocks by the storm, he wouldn't have run off and deserted his men. He, Jamie, was a man now and could no longer run away from responsibility.

Mrs. Wight must have been doing her own thinking. After a while she returned with the potatoes and plumped herself into her chair decisively.

"I've changed my mind, Heber," she announced. "You can try moving the house. I've been thinking to myself that if all those sealers trust you to get their ship through the ice safely, your own wife ought to trust you to sail a house across the bay. Shall I begin packing the dishes into boxes so they won't get broken?"

Getting the Wight house ready for the trip across the bay needed almost as much preparation as it had taken to outfit the *Polar Star* for her voyage to the icefields.

"What about the furniture?" asked Mrs. Wight.

"We'll leave some of it on the lower floor for ballast," said the captain. "The rest can go across in a trapboat."

All of the men in the village gave up their inshore fishing long enough to get the captain's house moved to the water.

As no mortar was used in the foundations for houses, it was

127

easy to pull out enough rocks to make room for support beams. Four great squared-off trunks of trees were run under the flooring and securely fastened.

"I've rounded up four pair of the strongest wagon wheels," reported Tom Boggan. "I'm sure that all together they'll bear the weight."

"If they don't," said the captain, "we'll slide her along on the wagon beds."

The wheels were set in axles fashioned on the ends of the beams. Then more rocks were dug from the foundation until the wheels rested on the ground.

But then the work was delayed by a heavy fog that moved in from the east. It settled over the houses and sheds of Spanish Choice Cove like a giant snowy owl brooding her eggs. Captain Wight fumed and studied his barometer. At last it promised clear weather.

It was a great day when two teams of horses were brought to pull the house on wheels. At dawn everyone in the village gathered at the Wight place to watch the novel sight.

There was always plenty of rope in a Newfoundland outport and "lashins" of it were needed. Lines were tied to the beams and the loose ends fastened to the harnesses of the horses.

"We'll put on a line for Sailor too," declared the captain. "This move is for him, so he should have some part in it."

They girdled the house with great nooses so that teams of men in the rear could cling to the ends to brake the house when necessary.

Everything was ready. The drivers waited at the horses' heads.

128

The brakemen took their stations in back. Sailor stood with his big red tongue hanging out expectantly.

"Weigh anchor, me boys!" shouted Captain Wight. "Full steam ahead!"

The horses strained and Sailor's chest swelled below his padded collar. Jamie and Meg put their hands to the spokes of a wheel as if working to get the fish wagon up the hill. Slowly the great wheels began to turn. The Wight house edged off its nest of rocks.

Down the road it creaked and jolted. It carried away part of a fence and knocked over a chicken coop, but like an invincible iceberg it kept on.

"It's going to upset," cried Mrs. Wight as the wheels on the right side rolled into a gully.

"She's listing to starboard!" shouted Captain Wight. "Heave taut on the port lines."

More men ran to the ropes on the left, and the house was steadied.

Near the village the road was blocked by an oncoming horse and buggy. The horse shied at sight of the moving house, and the buggy was nearly overturned in the ditch.

"Brake her!" shouted the captain.

The men in back pulled on the ropes until the house came to a stop. The driver jumped out of the buggy and hurried to his horse's head. He grabbed the bridle, then glared at the sight in the road. He was the dog constable.

"Heber Wight, what are you up to?" he asked as he recognized the captain and his house.

"And what are you up to, Constable Cotter?" asked the captain.

"It's the dog matter," stated the constable. "I have a warrant for him. You broke your word to me, Captain Wight, after you promised to take him away and find a new master."

"That I did, Constable Cotter," declared the captain. "I found a master for him. And I also told you that if things did not work out right, I'd jerk up my house and move it away. And that's exactly what I'm doing."

The constable stared at the house with a mixture of irritation and admiration.

"Heber Wight," he declared, "you are a remarkable man. When I said I believed you'd do it, I really didn't mean it."

"And I didn't mean it when I said I'd move the house," confessed the captain.

"However," said the constable, "I will not tear up the warrant and leave until I see your house afloat."

"Then you'll have to stay around for several hours until the tide comes in, William," said the captain. "And there's no reason you should idle the time away. Lend a hand on the port after line."

The constable hesitated a few seconds. Then he backed his skittish mare down the road to a clearing and made ready to tether her to a tree.

"We can use the horse too, on the starboard bow," shouted the captain.

The constable was so astonished at the position in which he found himself that he obediently unhitched his horse from the

130

buggy. He led her to the front of the house and the men teamed her with two bays. Then the constable pulled off his coat, hung it over an alder bush, and took his place on one of the braking ropes.

The house began to move again. The front ropes tautened going up the hills, and the rear ones on the descents. The house swayed on a turn but kept its balance.

When they reached the village, frightened chickens squawked and fled up the footpaths. Curious sheep, marked with red paint to identify their owners, followed the cortege to what the fishermen called the "lanch." It was a broad wooden slide that slanted down to the water. The fishermen used it for pulling up or launching boats and nets on crude sleds.

There was more conjecture and argument before the house could begin its hazardous descent. Although the water was already at low tide, men measured its depths to make sure that it would not come over the tops of their rubber boots when they would wade out for their final work. They compared the width of the lanch with that of the house so there would be a smooth descent.

The horses were freed from the ropes and their drivers joined the brakemen. Sailor bounded to Jamie and waited for praise.

The boy didn't disappoint him. "You're strong as a horse," he declared. "I bet you could pull that house all by yourself."

"Steeay!" cried Captain Wight at last. "Let her down easy. We don't want to wreck any of the flakes or stages."

The house started down the lanch. The men strained and shouted and tangled as they braked the descent. William

131

Cotter's face was red and his neck swollen from the unaccustomed physical exertion.

The wheels rumbled and squeaked down the wooden planks. They rolled out into the low water, then settled on the rocky bottom.

Quickly the men put on their boots and went to work with the empty barrels being rolled down the ramp. The barrels were nailed into place as floats all around the bottom of the house.

"You can help with the barrels too, William," said the captain to the constable. "It will be a long wait until the tide rises to float her."

The constable pushed back his round derby hat and wiped his sweating forehead. He looked ruefully at the grime on his trouser leg.

"I'll take your word that you're moving the dog away, Heber," he said. "I just remember that I have an important appointment back in Sample's Harbour."

He took the warrant from his back pocket and tore it into pieces. He tossed them down the lanch. "You must really think a lot of that dog" were his parting words as he went to his horse.

"It isn't that I think so much of the dog," shouted the captain, "as that Sarah thinks so much of her house."

While they waited for high tide the men went to their homes for midday dinner. The Wights and the children had theirs at the Boggans'. Aunt Maggie Boggan was noted for her partridge berry pies, and she had made a batch especially for the occasion.

While they were gone, the tide began to rise slowly. It licked higher and higher on the stilts of the rickety stages. It lapped

132

at the wharf pilings. It covered part of the wagon wheels. The barrels began to rise. By the middle of the afternoon, the house was rocking gently. It was afloat.

"She's seaworthy," boasted the captain. "I could put sails on her and head for the Labrador right now."

Towlines were fastened between the house and two longboats. Tom Boggan's skiff awaited its passengers and the boxes of dishes. A crew of men collected rope and horses and started on the long drive around the bay to meet the house and pull it up on land.

"A captain always sails with his ship," stated Captain Wight. "The rest of you get in Tom's boat."

"The house is my ship too," Mrs. Wight maintained. "I'm sailing on it with you."

Meg and Jamie begged to go with the house—Jamie wanted to sit on the roof and be the lookout—but the captain refused. "You young ones and Sailor ride with Tom," he ordered. "We can't be all captains and no crew."

"If the house sinks," said Jamie, "Sailor can rescue you and Mrs. Wight like he done me."

"It is a tradition of the sea that a captain goes down with his ship," announced Captain Wight. "And, be cripes, I'll go down with her before I'll listen to Sarah's reproaches for the rest of my life."

"Now, Heber," remonstrated Mrs. Wight, "I married you for better or worse, and I'm making this move for better or worse and come what may."

As the yellow house with the green trim was towed to sea by

133

sturdy men rowing the longboats, the villagers gathered on stages and wharf to give a gay send-off. Old Uncle Charlie Butler even shot off his gun in salute.

Captain and Mrs. Wight waved from an upstairs window. Then the captain left his post. "I'm going below to see how things are," he explained.

As soon as he reached the kitchen, he saw a trickle of water coming from under a closet door.

"Woe upon us!" he shouted up the steps. "She's taking on water from the closet. Come get your mop, Sarah."

Mrs. Wight anxiously descended the swaying staircase. "It's that mouse hole," she cried. "I meant to tell you about it."

The captain swung the closet door open and a flood of water gushed over the kitchen linoleum. He quickly grabbed a dish-towel, and reaching into the gurgling pool, stuffed the hole securely.

Sea gulls wheeled and dived over the Wight house. Schools of fish swam under it. Two lone men in a boat looked up in astonishment from their fishing poles.

"Must be a ferry off course," said one.

"Didn't hear nothing about a flood," commented the other.

A few hundred yards off shore Sailor jumped over the gunwale of Tom's boat and swam for the beach.

At last the oarsmen beached their longboats and pulled on the towlines. The house floated toward the sandy beach.

Captain Wight studied the shoreline with his spyglass.

"The teams are nearing Sample's Harbour," he announced. "It will be a little while before they get here. Bring us ashore, Tom, and we'll look around."

The Wights opened the front door and stepped into Tom's boat. The children made room for them.

When the bow crunched on the beach, Sailor was already ashore. He raced for the waterfall and began splashing under it.

"That dog never seems to get enough water," commented Tom.

Captain Wight put his arm around Sarah and led her to the finished foundation. "There's the bottom of your new home, Sarah," he announced.

"It looks bigger than the house," said Mrs. Wight.

"Had to make it wide enough for the new room I'm going to build on."

"Look, Jamie," Meg pointed. "There sets our school on the outside of Sample's Harbour. We won't have far to go."

The children joined the Wights. Mrs. Wight put an arm around each. "What's the name of this cove?" she asked her husband.

"It's got no name as far as I know," replied the captain.

Jamie looked at Sailor frisking under the waterfall and snapping at the spray.

"Yes, it has," he said. "It's Sailor's Choice Cove."

136

Glossary

Glossary

airsome—cold and stormy

ballycatters—heavy shore ice

bedlamer—three-year-old harp seal

brewis—stew of hard biscuit and meat or fish, pronounced "broose"

duff—pudding made of flour, fat pork, and water

elsinor—warm cap with ear muffs

flakes—platforms or ground where fish are dried

fruz—mixed-up state

garagee—free-for-all fight

gurry—oil and blood from seal pelts

hounds—old squaw ducks whose calls are believed by some to sound
      like the baying of hounds

jackeen—rascally boy

jinkers—persons who bring bad luck

knobbly—rough

nunny bag—small canvas bag

outport—small settlement on coast

pinnacle—peak of ice

rallies—seal hunts on ice

sculp—skin of seal with adhering layer of fat

sculping—peeling sculp from body of seal with knife

scutters—hind flippers of seal

shule—to back up

sidesticks—long poles held by ropes which are hung over sides of ship in ladderlike fashion

slindge—to evade work

swile—seal

swiling—hunting seals